Ailsa and Alf were out that Sunday when Roo made her foray into the house behind the supermarket . . . It would seem that it was quite a simple matter for Roo to gain entry into the house, although the method by which this was achieved remains obscure. But gain entry she did; snoop around she did; find something of extreme interest she also did in the course of her stealthy examination, for which there can be no excuse, but then, of course, the girl's determination knew no bounds of what was the right thing to do and what was wrong. She was intent only on finding evidence that would be incriminating enough to put an end to her father's marriage plans.

Also available from Mandarin Paperbacks

Home and Away Vol 2

Home and Away™

SUMMER BAY BLUES

Thames Mandarin

A Thames Mandarin Paperback

HOME AND AWAY

First published in Great Britain 1990
by Mandarin Paperbacks
Michelin House, 81 Fulham Road, London SW3 6RB
in association with
Thames Television International Limited
149 Tottenham Court Road, London WIP 9LL

Mandarin is an imprint of the Octopus Publishing Group

Novel © W H Allen 1990
Cover photography by Steven Brack

Registered Trademark – Autralian Television Network
1987

A CIP catalogue record for this title
is available from the British Library

ISBN 0 7493 0712 9

Printed and bound in Great Britain
by Cox & Wyman Ltd, Reading, Berks

One

Our town is aptly named; it's always summer in Summer Bay, that's what they like to say, except in the winter and even then the weather's not so bad for most of the time, sunny days, a bit cool maybe, although those north-easterly winds can be a bit of a bother when they come shrieking over the headland straight into the bay. There are also periods of rain, and occasional storms which whip up the surf and there's a constant roar and a rumble as the waves crash down on the beach, eating right into it so there's always this problem of erosion, with the beach getting narrower and narrower, about half the width it was, twenty years ago, and there's the worry about those houses further around the bay that are perched right on the edge of it. One of these days, they say, one of these days, a particularly ferocious storm . . . It's definitely on the cards if they don't do something about it, and soon. Anyway, when those sharp north-easterlies come hurtling over the point and whistle along the esplanade everyone has to bend almost double as they hurry off into it and all the windows and doors rattle in their frames and the air is full of stinging sea-spray.

There are those people who say they prefer the town during those winter months, if the weather's reasonable, when it's not so busy, not so rushed as it is in the summer when the people come up from the city for their holidays, and the beach is crowded, and it's almost impossible to find a parking spot anywhere along the esplanade where the shops are. Not that it isn't good for business, all these people milling about on holiday, or just up for the weekend, buying things at prices that have been suitably adjusted for that busy season to make up for when times are slack – well, a couple of the shops, anyway; it's common knowledge. But after all that, when things settle down again and life gets back to normal, it's really a quiet little place. The fishing boats set out early and come back late; there are always a few board riders lying out there beyond the breakers in their wet suits, waiting to catch a good wave no matter what the weather's like; there's the pub up by the lagoon which is always popular, and the bowling club where the beer is cheaper. There are a couple of motels, one or two restaurants, the usual run of shops, the school, the police station, the post office, the two churches and so on.

Like every small town that seems quiet enough on the surface, there's always something happening – and while everyone knows everyone else, more or less, there are those who know *about* everyone else, more or less, who are well up with the local gossip, all the dramas, the love affairs, who's getting divorced, who had a skinful and rolled his car, things like that. Now and again something comes up to set the tongues wagging for days or weeks on end, something a bit more juicy than the run of the mill squabbles and romances, road works, council rates, the horse races, football, the weather, the day's fishing catch and such like – grist for the mill, you might say, for those evening discussions that take place in either the pub or the bowling club, or wherever for that matter, so that everyone is kept abreast of the latest developments, or if there are no developments filling in a little here and there, making a few guesses, offering a theory or two because, as they say, no one likes a mystery.

Again like any small town, you've got your different types of characters to make it more interesting. There are some people who are popular and some people who are unpopular, like that grim-faced school headmaster, Donald Fisher, a divorced man who is always on at the kids about something or other, maybe working off his frustrations, because he looks like a man who would have plenty of them to work off – a pursed-up sort of person, if that makes any sense. But then again, maybe there has to be a line drawn with those kids, or some of them at least, so they don't get away with murder, to lay down the law and not let them get to you like they got to old Bertram who was the headmaster before him – or maybe old Bertram had a screw loose before the kids got to him and he would have gone stalking around the place in the middle of the night, anyway, frightening the life out of people, making strange telephone calls and muttering about the wrath of God and similar threats, starting fires and poisoning Nico Poletti's pet cow who was deficient in a couple of screws himself and likely to go berserk for no reason anyone could think of, like he did when his pet cow was poisoned. Poor old Bertram – he was very docile when they led him away. Nico got himself another cow in the end, and for a while things quietened down in the town.

So you've got your popular people and your unpopular people; you've got your successful people and those who have had their run of bad luck, and a reasonable example in that category would be Tom and Pippa Fletcher who haven't been all that long in the town, having moved up the coast from the city after Tom was retrenched from his job, a victim of technology and these inflationary times no doubt, although there could have been other reasons no one knows about. Anyway, they're here now, in Summer Bay, and maybe they did think that the caravan park would be a sound investment, and it still could be, even though it's a little run down, it just needs a bit of work done to it, which Tom has been doing, but that's about all he's been doing because apart from a couple of regulars, the place just isn't making any money, which is a worry, particularly with those kids of theirs who are not really their own kids but ones they've taken in to foster although now it turns out that Pippa is pregnant which is even more of a worry. Even in Summer Bay one cannot just live on fresh air and sunshine which, of course, is healthier than living in the city. So there they are with Tom doing odd jobs around the caravan park, and even though there's hardly any money coming in he's dead against Pippa, who was once a nurse at one of the city hospitals, going back to work. He wouldn't have that at all. If anyone was going back to work, *he* would be the one – and in any case, what was she talking about? She was expecting, wasn't she, and no one should be going to work when they are expecting. Tom has his pride, no doubt about it. Even when Ailsa Hogan who runs the local supermarket suggested that she and Pippa open up a café of some description together, he hummed and hawed and showed an even greater lack of confidence. Still and all, everything considered and in the long run, Tom and Pippa probably came up here at the right time, even though there are those who say they came up here at the wrong time, there being pessimists everywhere, even in Summer Bay, and picked up that run-down caravan park comparatively cheap, because judging by the gleam in certain property developers' eyes, our coastal town has great tourist potential – but more about that later, except to point out now that Tom and Pippa and their caravan park are sitting on a prime piece of real estate between the lagoon and the Pacific Coast.

When Ailsa brought up her idea of opening a café in partnership with Pippa, she most probably would have discussed it beforehand with Alf Stewart who operates the local liquor store, because the two of them are at the point that there would have been wedding bells before now except for the fly in the ointment that goes by the name of Roo, this being Alf's daughter who has been showing some reluctance about having Ailsa as a stepmother and apparently does everything she can to throw a spanner in the works of this otherwise smooth-running romance, putting on fits of temperament and the like whenever the subject comes up for discussion, which doesn't happen so much these days because of the unpleasantness it arouses which means that Alf has to take to measures of subterfuge to keep the fact that he is still seeing Ailsa from her. Alf, who is a widower, thinks the world of Roo (whose real name is Ruth but everyone calls her Roo, that being a sort of nickname), and he doesn't want to hurt her, which places him in something of a predicament because he thinks the world of Ailsa, too, and doesn't want to hurt her, while Ailsa, in her turn, thinks the world of him and is not at all happy about the situation – or that's the general opinion on the matter.

It is only natural that this is the subject of some lively gossip in the town, a lot of it supplied by Alf's sister,

Celia, a real scatterbrain that one, always putting her nose in where she shouldn't, never doing anything right and making a thorough nuisance of herself. She never married, the story being that she had been engaged once but her fiancée was killed in action during the Vietnam war, but she felt she had a talent for match-making which in the case of Alf and Ailsa reached such a point that Alf finally had to take a stand by telling Ailsa that he wanted to cool their relationship, which Ailsa didn't appreciate in the slightest; for a few days afterwards she was walking around with a sort of preoccupied expression. Then, when she started looking happy again and could be heard actually singing as she refilled the shelves in her supermarket, it wasn't hard to guess what had happened, the course of true love being what it is Alf and Ailsa had put the seal on their feelings for each other by announcing their engagement.

That done, having decided on their engagement, the next important thing was to let Roo, or Ruth, in on the arrangement, let her know that the die was cast and that nothing could be changed once they had made up their minds to become engaged and that Alf had probably already bought the ring if he was not still giving serious consideration to this necessity. Anyway – so the story has it – the girl Ruth, or Roo, was furious when faced with this announcement of their plans, she wasn't going to take it lying down, and if there was a way to stop it from going ahead she vowed to herself with savage intensity that she would find it. For this she sought the assistance of her Aunt Celia who, it seemed, now had her own axe to grind, having received a stinging rebuff from Ailsa when she became too intrusive in the matter of the broken romance which turned out to be not broken at all. Nobody knows what did actually pass between them during this encounter, but Ailsa can be pretty much down to earth when she sets her mind to it, and Roo's Aunt Celia with her airs and graces, her church-going and moral attitudes, her genteel refinement and all the rest of the show, must have been quite put out when Ailsa told her in no uncertain terms what she thought of the sister of the man to whom she had become engaged.

Now the thing about Ailsa was that no one in the town knew much about her, since she has not been with us in our seaside community for very long. As her fiancé and prospective husband, it might be thought that Alf at least probably knew enough of what was needed to know about her past, but as for the rest . . . On this subject, even Celia, normally so full of information about everyone and everything around the place, had no opinion to offer, informed or otherwise. Now, with Roo as an accomplice, this was something she resolved to put right.

The most direct way of finding something out about a person is to go up to that person with a list of questions you would like to have answered about their former activities, and it was fair enough for Celia and Roo to show some understandable curiosity about this imminent addition to the family, just as it was fair enough for that person who was the subject of such interest to be forthcoming and frank about those said activities. But in this case, as it was to be learned by medium of Celia, her future sister-in-law was strangely reticent about those matters they wanted to know about. In other words which probably explain it better, she was neither forthcoming nor frank. In fact, so she reported to Roo, Celia had the distinct impression that Ailsa was being cagey, which only served to stimulate their curiosity even more, that being only natural under the circumstances. No one likes to be faced with a mystery, which was what Ailsa was turning out to be. So, smelling the proverbial rat, Roo set out on the trail of discovery which led, in the first instance, to Ailsa's house behind the supermarket, not a great distance by any means of calculation.

Ailsa and Alf were out that Sunday afternoon when Roo made her foray into the house behind the supermarket. They had gone picnicking to one of those areas for which our region is justifiably noted, the National Park, which stretches for many miles along the coastline north of our town. It would seem that it was quite a simple matter for Roo to gain entry into the house, although the method by which this was achieved remains obscure. But gain entry she did; snoop around she did; find something of extreme interest she also did in the course of her stealthy examination, for which there can be no excuse, but then, of course, the girl's determination knew no bounds of what was the right thing to do and what was wrong. She was intent only on finding evidence that would be incriminating enough to put an end to her father's marriage plans.

What she did find during her search, probably in one of the drawers, although it's just useless speculation to wonder where she did find it, it could have been lying on a table or even in a wastepaper basket, or anywhere, was a letter or a card of an unmistakably romantic content, although the details of what was written on that card or in that letter were never made explicit. That was interesting enough, but what was even more interesting was

12

that this communication was written by Donald Fisher who took over as headmaster after old Bertram went round the bend and thought everyone was persecuting him which was why he started persecuting everyone else, a strange and worrying situation at the time. It was probably easy for Roo to put two and two together, seeing the signature Donald or Don on this letter and being familiar with the handwriting of the headmaster at her school. It was an eye-opener; until that time no one had any idea that there were such goings-on between Ailsa and the headmaster. Yes, there was definitely more to Ailsa, this dark horse, than met the eye.

Celia thought so, too, when Roo told her of her discovery, and decided that if anyone could unearth more facts about Ailsa's past it would be her sister, Morag, in the city, where she was some sort of leading light in the legal profession, a Supreme Court judge no less, and a cold and superior type of woman at that. Morag would have the means at her disposal to set the necessary enquiries in train; she would be just as concerned about what her brother might be letting himself in for by committing himself to Ailsa for the rest of his life as Celia and Roo were. Of course, everyone had Alf's interests at heart; they were very concerned about him.

But here, while Celia was apprising her sister, Morag, of the facts, a complication developed for Roo in which she found herself put severely at risk. The tables were turned, you might say, when the letter she had taken from Ailsa's house was discovered in her school locker by Bobby Simpson – and this is really how the whole affair became public knowledge, much to the embarrassment of Ailsa and Donald Fisher.

There was no love lost between these two girls,

Roo and Bobby Simpson whose real name is probably Roberta, but everyone calls her Bobby. Bobby is a tough little nut who, before she had been taken in by the Stewarts – that is when Mrs Stewart was still alive – had apparently spent some time in a reform school. Another thing about Bobby is that she has an unsettling effect on the boys of this town, and that's putting it mildly. Anyway, the first thing she did when she found the letter was to confront Ailsa with it. Naturally, Ailsa was furious at what she regarded as this invasion of her privacy. Things looked pretty grim for Roo there for a while.

It seems that while there might have been something between Donald Fisher and Ailsa at one time, a spark ignited by the fact that Ailsa was living alone and Donald Fisher is a divorced man, this had finished quite some time ago because, as Ailsa explained it to Bobby Simpson who had confronted her with the letter, she realized that Donald Fisher possessed some characteristics she didn't find attractive, a not uncommon observation whenever the subject of the school headmaster comes up for discussion.

What Ailsa does then is call Roo's bluff. She puts it squarely on the line. Okay, she says thrusting the letter back at her, you go right ahead and tell Alf about Donald and me, it's all history now, anyway, and then you tell him how you found out about it, by snooping around in my house when you had no right to be there, after breaking and entering, which is against the law. There would have been more in this vein, Ailsa spitting out her words, making her meaning sharp and clear, and Roo was forced to face up to the fact that her father would hit the roof when he learned what she had done.

In short, she was given food for thought as a result of this encounter with an irate Ailsa.

Nor was Bobby Simpson prepared to let up on the pressure, given her feelings for Alf, whom she regarded as a father and, who in fact had been a father to her. And then, too, there was Ailsa whom she cared about very much and whose happiness was being threatened by Roo's actions. At school the next day, before classes began, there was another confrontation, a notable clash; Bobby is not one for the subtle approach, she's more inclined to just lash out and say what she thinks which in this case was quite a great deal. One thing leading to another, a tussle developed and a crowd gathered. It turned out to be a real screaming match, with some hair pulled, some punches thrown, a scratch or two inflicted – and in the middle of all this frenzy, just before it was broken up by Donald Fisher who marched the two combatants off to his office to lay down the law and hand out weekend detentions for such unruly behaviour, the incriminating letter was somehow dropped, only to be picked up later by one of the interested bystanders who proved eager to share the information so gained. That was how the word got around the school that morning to the accompaniment of much sniggering and suggestive speculation, and why Donald Fisher, coming to hear about it soon enough, rushed straight round to Ailsa's supermarket to demand what the hell was going on.

Ailsa told him nothing; her ignorance on the subject was complete. She probably did convince him in the end that she had no idea how this thing had leaked out before he went away still looking worried.

With the word now spreading, Ailsa decided she should tell Alf about this past involvement of hers, no matter how temporary it had been, before he heard it from someone else which would have been inevitable if she let it go too long. So she told him; earnestly she explained the extent of the involvement, which had been terminated with no chance of it being renewed, because of the warmth of the feelings she now had for Alf. It had been a short fling, that was all, something fleeting and of no significance whatever, past history now. Naturally enough, Alf was a little hurt that she hadn't told him about it before; complete and utter frankness was something he would have expected from his future bride, because trust is essential in such a relationship. But – and presumably here he gave a philosophic shrug, smiled bravely and showed in other ways the forgivingness of the nature of a man whose intended had just informed him of her short-lived affair with the local headmaster – the past was the past, the future was theirs and theirs alone with no interlopers, hopefully, to mar the domestic scene, which is a good and positive attitude to take. Anyway, now that this revelation was out of the system, they could go ahead with the plans for the engagement party – in all ignorance that this happy occasion would be thrown into turmoil by Roo's announcement, relayed from her Aunt Morag in the city who had telephoned her with the news only that morning, that Ailsa's past life included a conviction for murder.

TWO

The National Park to the north of our town has already been mentioned. Actually, it extends many miles to the north along the coast until it reaches the river mouth on the far side of which stands the State's second largest seaport; and inland, covering a huge expanse of bush and roughly in the shape of a wedge with its base on the river and to where the new highway loops back in towards the coast. To the south of us there are more beaches and townships of varying sizes and conditions, beginning with Yabbie Creek which stands on the creek behind the hills that enclose our own town of Summer Bay. To reach Yabbie Creek, the road winds up out of the esplanade fronting the beach and doubles back above the town before veering away and down the other side. In the opposite direction the road negotiates a small bluff then continues on out past the lagoon past orchards and farmland, to connect up with the highway about ten miles away.

Because it seems comparatively cut-off and isolated, it's not the sort of place where you'd think there would be too many lurking dangers – and it's not really. People still tend to leave their doors unlocked when they leave their houses for short periods of time, and they even trust strangers. Whatever crime does exist in the town is generally of the minor variety, the occasional pilfering perhaps, but more likely drivers exceeding the speed limit, driving under the influence, negligently or without a licence, and the odd violence like domestic trouble, or the result of a drunken altercation or maybe bad feeling over some girl or other – which happens sometimes, particularly on a Saturday night when the pub does a roaring trade – none of this is of such a seriousness as to have Bob Barnett, our local constable, call for reinforcements on the telephone, although it must be said that he was scratching his head in perplexity for a while there when old Bertram, the former headmaster, was up to his strange and unnerving tricks before anyone knew it *was* old Bertram who was up to them.

Major crime, like murder, armed robbery, kidnapping, assault and battery or drug-dealing is generally unknown in this largely law-abiding community. A motor accident in the district is a sensation, particularly if they're locals and you know the people involved, which is often the case – more so, of course, if the pile-up results in fatalities. But as far as crime – that is real crime – goes, there's not much of it, and when it does happen then people react more than those who live surrounded by it all the time, like they do in the city. It's closer to home, you feel the repercussions more because it's such a small community. Like the time when young Carly Morris, one of the foster children who had been taken in by Tom and Pippa Fletcher when she was younger, was attacked that night when she did a silly thing and decided to hitch-hike back from Yabbie Creek instead of doing the sensible thing and waiting for the late bus that leaves shortly after the pictures are over and would have dropped her right at the caravan park where she lived. Even in our area the kids had been warned about the dangers of accepting lifts from strangers – and at the school Donald Fisher is particularly hot on that sort of thing, always drumming it into the kids' heads that they should never accept lifts from strangers under any circumstances because that is only inviting trouble. But Carly is a headstrong girl; she hitched a ride home that night after she'd had an argument with that kid Matt, the bronzed surfer, with whom she had gone to the movies, and run out on him in a fit of anger, only to get herself into deeper trouble by accepting a lift from some guy she didn't know.

She didn't let on at first what had happened, she kept it to herself, but it was plain to all those around her that she was upset about something, tense, brittle and close to tears. She wouldn't let anyone touch her, even Matt, who wanted to make up the quarrel that had sent her running off into the night after the pictures were over. But then it did come out in the end; she finally blurted it out to the other kids of the Fletcher household who were demanding to know what was wrong with her, and why she was carrying on like that all of a sudden with her fits of shivering and blank stares off into the distance.

She told them what had happened that night. She told them that she had relived it over and over again since then, even dreaming about it, so she would wake up drenched with perspiration and with a stifled scream on her lips. She described how she had flung herself out of the car when it pulled off the road onto a side track and she had immediately known what was about to happen, and about the wild chase through the bush when she had heard him crashing through the undergrowth behind her, steadily gaining on her . . . It was still very close to her, still very painful to relive those events one more time while the others listened to her story in shocked silence.

It was still painful as they sat around and discussed what they should do, and it was put to the vote whether Tom and Pippa should be told and the police notified which was what Carly didn't want because of her fear of the malicious gossip that would ensue if the story became public. She pleaded and argued, and finally persuaded them to accept her point of view. Best leave things as they are, she insisted; all she wanted to do was put the incident out of her mind, although she did concede that if she saw the man again she would be quite prepared to kill him, so full of hatred was she for what he had done to her.

It might have stayed that way if one of Carly's foster-sisters, Lynn, who had been the first to support Carly's wish not to have the matter made public because of the scandal that would bring, didn't go through something of a religious crisis as a result of the events just described and began to show disturbing signs of cynicism during her confirmation classes which became quite a worry to Father Damien who conducted them. When she stopped going to the classes altogether, Father Damien was concerned enough to approach Tom Fletcher about the matter, pointing out that while he didn't want to interfere in the often touchy subject of a family's reli-gious activities he did think it a little strange that Lynn seemed to have now a sudden change of heart as far as her religious instruction was concerned. Tom, too, thought it was curious and offered himself to Lynn as a person always ready and willing to listen to any problems she might have.

Someone else who was concerning herself with Lynn's

religious welfare was Alf Stewart's sister, Celia, who became so persistent in her efforts to get Lynn to go back to church that Lynn, obviously breaking down under the strain of this continued pressure, gave vent to what was troubling her. How could there be a God? she demanded (to Celia's horror because Celia is a fervent church-going woman for whom such questions simply do not arise). How can I believe in a God, Lynn wailed miserably, who allows Carly to be raped?

There now, the awful truth revealed. It had come out without thinking, spilled out in a torrent of rage and frustration, the shocking fact imparted to a woman who, with her reputation as the town gossip, was in a position to wreak the most havoc with the information. Lynn was appalled by what she had done in a moment of thoughtlessness, but there was no way she could take her words back. The damage had been done.

In a panic by now, Lynn rushed off to see Bobby Simpson who had also supported Carly against those who had wanted to report the attack on her to the police and whose reaction now was to hurry to Alf Stewart in the hope that he could head his meddlesome sister off at the pass before she could spread the story any further – a forlorn hope as it turned out; thanks to Celia, the cat was already well and truly out of the bag, and everybody knew, or was about to know, what had happened that night.

Alf was furious with his sister for her interference, which this time, he shouted, had gone too far and could quite possibly have scarred Carly for life – and if she had any scruples at all, which he doubted, she should apologize to the kid for being so selfish and stupid as to go running off to her friends with the news she had just heard. From all accounts, Alf was really mad, and Celia was suitably admonished for her impetuosity (which was certainly nothing new). Even so, she did spend a sleepless and fretful night in the realization of what she had done, and in the morning promised her brother that she would see Carly that very day and apologize.

If Lynn and Bobby had hoped to break the news to Tom and Pippa before they heard it from anyone else, they were again too late, Pippa had already been told about it by Mrs Smart who can never keep her mouth shut about anything under the sun, the juicier the scandal the better because that is just the sort of thing to give her a renewed lease of life. Much of Tom's anger was directed towards the kids who thought they could handle such a serious matter by themselves, he blamed his oldest foster-son, Frank, in particular because Frank was old enough to have a sense of responsibility and know better – which is a bit of an irony because Frank was the one who had insisted on them going to the police in the first place before he was out-voted by the others. In the meantime, Tom had already been to see Bob Barnett, the town policeman, who hadn't been too encouraging about Carly's attacker being found because it was clear that he wasn't a local man.

Poor Carly – in the middle of all this uproar she stepped forward and told them that she was the one to blame, no one else; she had begged the others to remain silent because she had felt so ashamed by what had happened. She hadn't wanted anyone to know, not even Tom and Pippa who she now tried to make see the situation from her own point of view. Tom, his anger abated somewhat by now, was prepared to concede that there were always personal and practical considerations

22

in such circumstances, and frankly, it was difficult for him to know what to do for the best.

So the tongues wagged in the town and different points of view were expressed, not all of them by any means sympathetic to Carly and her ordeal. At school it was even worse, some of the other kids who were not so friendly towards her took advantage of her unhappiness by openly taunting her with remarks that basically boiled down to the suggestion that she might not have been backward in encouragement that night when she had accepted a lift from a total stranger – the slander invited some fierce tussles in the school yard before, between and after classes, and resulted in some minor physical damage to the perpetrators.

Inside the school itself, Donald Fisher, the headmaster, decided to use Carly's experience as an object lesson to the other pupils bearing out his repeated warnings about putting themselves in the same position as Carly had done – but then, as he was lecturing them on the evils and pitfalls of hitch-hiking and being too trusting of strangers, Carly interrupted him and regained much of the respect she had lost by frankly acknowledging her own stupidity for which she had already suffered enough and which she didn't want anyone else to experience. This gave force and immediacy to Donald Fisher's observations which, like much else about the man, would not have been exactly compelling.

But Carly was still angry that the story had gotten around in the first place, and she vented this anger on Celia when she came to apologize that afternoon. Carly was bitter, and in no mood for reconciliation. She lashed out at the stunned Celia who could only stare at her with her mouth open as she was accused of being malicious

and troublemaking, a dessicated spinster whose only
purpose in life was to make life unbearable for everyone
else, which wasn't exactly fair on the woman who, in her
own ineffectual way, means well enough but treads on
everyone's toes nevertheless.

Three

Another form of violence one hears about now and again is that of the domestic variety, and a good example of this as far as Summer Bay is concerned was the case of Sandra Barlow, whose father would beat her up in a way you wouldn't believe and apparently for little or no reason other than that he was drunk at the time. A very unpleasant type was Sam Barlow, a nasty sneering type, and if there was enough tension around him outside his home it was plain there was even more inside the fibro walls of the house down by the narrow end of the lagoon, where he and his family lived.

Barlow worked for the local district council, in charge of the road gang on which Tom Fletcher was employed for a while until the day he knocked out Barlow during a brawl that followed on some snide comment Barlow had made about Carly. There had been bad blood between them from the beginning, and if it hadn't been Carly and her troubles it would have been something else that would have sparked the fuse. Tom was sacked but everyone was on his side. No one had any time for Sam Barlow, a drunk and a loudmouth if there ever was one, and they reckoned it was not before time that he got the comeuppance that had sent him sprawling in the dust.

At the time Sandra was friendly with young Steve Mathieson, yet another of the Fletcher tribe of foster-children, and a kid, incidentally, with a tragic background: both his parents were trapped inside their house after it caught fire and Steve, then very little, had managed to escape the blaze somehow, a scene he recalls with frightening vividness and will probably remember until the end of his days, such a shocking and traumatic experience it had been. Although he's still only fifteen or so and there's plenty of time yet for the wounds to heal over to leave only the scars which sometimes fade until they become quite indistinct.

Anyway, Steve was friendly with Sandra Barlow, but this friendship was restricted only to school hours because there was no way that her father would allow Sandra to keep company with Steve or any other boy, because they had only one thing on their mind as far as girls were concerned, meaning he was probably drawing on his own experiences when he was the same age. He kept his eyes on her like a hawk, and had already warned Steve to keep his distance, barging into school one day after everyone else had gone home and Steve was helping Sandra with a science project which was proving quite difficult for her. Barlow had been most irate to find the two of them alone together, hunched over the science project, and, red in the face, shaking his fist and raising his voice, had threatened Steve with what would happen to him if he kept seeing his daughter because he knew exactly what Steve was after. This was a bit unfair because all Steve was doing was helping Sandra with her science project and probably hadn't anything like what Barlow was suggesting in mind. Barlow's aggressiveness had been quite alarming to the boy, who could see by her expression how frightened Sandra was of her father as he virtually dragged her out of the classroom.

The next morning, when Sandra turned up at school with a swollen eye, Steve, who had already decided that if they couldn't work on the science project after school then it would have to be before school and was ready to suggest this to her when she arrived, was even more alarmed. He pressed her on the subject of the swollen eye – When? How? Why? – but the more persistent he was about it the more angry she became. Leave off, she snapped, close to tears; it was nothing to do with him, not his problem at all; she refused to discuss it and walked away leaving the matter of the science project still unresolved, and Steven more perplexed and worried than ever.

After school was over for the day, Steve intercepted Sandra and offered to walk home with her. But Sandra was reluctant about this and showed some apprehension which lessened only slightly when Steve assured her that it would be all right, no problem, because her father was still at work with the road gang, wasn't he, and wouldn't be home for more than a couple of hours yet – which should have been true. What Steve didn't know, couldn't possibly know, having been in school all day, was that the men on the road gang had gone on strike for some reason or other, which was why Barlow came home unexpectedly early while Steve was sitting with Sandra in the kitchen, discussing the school science project. Fortunately for Steve, Sandra managed to hustle him out of the back door when she heard her father's footsteps on the front porch, then the sound of the key turning in the lock of the front door. It was a close call; Steve didn't want to think about what would have happened if Barlow had found him there after his savage threats of the previous day. As he hurried away towards the reeds that fringed the lagoon at the rear of the house, he carried with him the sharp image of the terror he had seen on Sandra's face at the realization that her father was home earlier than either of them had expected.

Back home, he tried to discuss his concern for Sandra with Tom Fletcher, his foster-father, but Tom had his own problems now, after his dust-up with Barlow and his subsequent dismissal from his job with the road-gang. Steve was almost desperate; he still tried to get Tom to share his worry that Sandra was being ill-treated by her father, but Tom wasn't having any part of it. There was enough bad blood between him and Barlow as it was, and in any event there was nothing he or anyone could do about it if Steve's fears did prove to be correct, as it was purely and simply a family matter and no one had any right to interfere in the domestic concerns of other people. Steve wasn't so sure about that; he had seen Sandra's swollen eye and the expression of terror on her face when she had heard her father's footsteps on the front porch that afternoon. There must be *something* one could do, he thought unhappily, it just wasn't right that a girl like Sandra should have to live in fear of her father. Steve spent a restless night just worrying about it.

In the morning, when he saw her at school, Sandra was tight-lipped and uncommunicative when Steve queried her about what had happened after her father returned home. She said nothing; she refused to say anything; she kept shaking her head and telling him nothing happened, everything was all right, so please don't keep on about it. Steve was left with the impression that she was protecting her father; her denials certainly didn't make him feel any easier.

It wasn't only Sandra who bore the brunt of Barlow's bad temper but her long-suffering mother as well, a fact which was common knowledge in the town where most people felt sorry for this poor woman, looking tired and aged beyond her years, who had put up with this treatment for so long. But she never complained; she was always loyal to her husband who, heaven only knew, scarcely deserved it, although it's possible he did have his good points that no one else knew about, or maybe she was desperately hanging on to the memory of better days. Who knows about these things, anyway? Who knows how much a person can endure in the, mostly, forlorn hope that matters might improve?

In this case, they weren't improving at all; if anything they were becoming steadily worse, so much so that when Sandra arrived home from school one afternoon to find that her mother wasn't there and that there were signs that a scuffle of some sort had taken place, then discovered a note written by her father to inform her that her mother had had a bad fall and had to be taken to hospital, she shed all her previous restraint and rushed straight round to see Ailsa Hogan, whose support she felt she could expect, given the circumstances. She didn't really want to involve Ailsa, but she felt she had no alternative; she was frightened of her father and didn't want to be alone with him. Ailsa understood that only too well; she had every reason. Returning to the Barlow house with Sandra, she found that the girl's parents had already returned, Mrs Barlow looking a little battered and bruised and totally subdued as always, particularly in the presence of her spouse who had now adopted his attitude of familial concern which didn't convince anyone for a moment, certainly not Ailsa whose distrust of such attitudes went back a very long way. But sceptical as she might be, there was nothing she could do or say except look at him a little narrowly when he placed his arm around his wife who had already agreed that, yes, she did have a very bad fall, she had somehow managed to lose her footing.

When the examinations came round, Sandra did quite well with the science project into which she and Steve had put so much work; what she didn't do so well with was her history assignment which immediately dashed Sam Barlow's satisfaction with her science results when she informed him and unsuccessfully tried to slip the poor history showing past him. Experiencing yet another of his violent changes of mood, he immediately lashed out at her, called her everything under the sun, and his yelling could be heard out on the street which was not uncommon when Barlow was in one of his rages. This time it was too much; she couldn't take any more of it. She was stirred up; Sandra yelled right back at him, crying out about how much she hated him before running right out of the house and making a beeline for Ailsa Hogan's residence behind the supermarket where, in tears, breaking down completely, she vowed never to return to that house where there was so much unhappiness. Ailsa was worried; she tried her best to console the girl, who woefully announced her intention of putting herself up for fostering, that was how desperate she had become, but at the same time attempted to make her see reason by saying that without any real evidence of abuse, something she could show that would prove the severity of the treatment she was receiving, there was little that could be done. With that, Sandra was suddenly seized with a new resolve that was a little alarming to Ailsa when she gave more thought to it after the girl had gone. She had left with an expression that could only be described as grimly determined – and the more Ailsa thought about it the more worried she became because it seemed to her that Sandra had made up her mind to force the issue, and the one way of doing that was to provoke her father into supplying her with enough bruises to give substance to her story of ill-treatment. Suddenly frightened for the girl, Ailsa grabbed hold of Alf Stewart from the liquor store, and both of them rushed around to the Barlow house in the hope that Ailsa's suspicions were wrong and, if they were not, that they wouldn't be too late to prevent serious injury or worse.

As they soon discovered, Ailsa's suspicions were not wrong, and they were too late because they had no sooner arrived at the house, quite out of breath, than Sam Barlow appeared at the door with a worried expression and announced in a choked voice that there had been an accident, Sandra had slipped and fallen in that house full of pitfalls where people seemed to be in the habit of losing their balance. She was unconscious, having struck her head rather badly on a corner of the table when she fell, and he had just telephoned for an ambulance to take her to the hospital at Loxton, which is a largish town a few miles beyond Yabbie Creek.

It was pathetic to see, the way he paced up and down outside that hospital room where Sandra was being kept under observation for suspected internal injuries, that vigil he maintained while Sandra flatly refused to see him despite her mother's pleas to let him come into the room because he was desperately worried about her, she had to give him a chance, he really *was* improving and in any case, Sandra had to admit that he had behaved the way he had because she had provoked him so badly. But Sandra was grimly adamant, she was prepared to give him no chance at all, she had the evidence now, they wouldn't let her go back home after what she had just suffered at her father's hands. No, no, she insisted, she was quite prepared to see this thing through, tell her story to the police who would then see to it that she was made a ward of the State, which would find her a suitable home in which she could be fostered. Hearing this, and aware that Mrs Barlow was unlikely to corroborate her daughter's story, Ailsa was in no way confident that this would be the outcome at all.

While this discussion was going on inside the hospital room, Sam Barlow was becoming more and more agitated out in the corridor. Why, he demanded, was he not being allowed to see his daughter? No one could give him any sort of an answer that would satisfy him, and it was finally Bob Barnett, our local constable, who had a quiet word in his ear and told him he wasn't taken in by all this paternal concern he was showing, that he was well aware of what had really happened, which put Barlow immediately onto the defensive. No one could pin anything on him – that was his attitude. There was no way anyone could make out a case against him.

A frequent visitor to Sandra while she was in hospital was young Steve Mathieson who brought her flowers and chocolates, and showed his concern when she expressed her fear of soon having to leave the safety of the hospital room and return home where she would once more be vulnerable. Deeply worried about what might happen to her, Steve sought out Barlow in a last-ditch attempt to salvage the situation, but as much as he talked and tried to make him see reason – in effect asked Barlow to give his daughter a break because she was terrified of him – he might as well have been talking to a brick wall. Barlow's reaction was typical; he told the kid to clear out and not bother himself over matters that didn't concern him. His tone was gruff and menacing. When Steve persisted because, no matter what Barlow thought, he was concerned about Sandra for whom he had developed strong feelings which he could tell from the way she looked at him sometimes, or spoke to him, were reciprocated. He felt very protective towards her; he didn't want to see her life ruined by this brute of a father. He hung on; he was tenacious; he demanded reassurance from Sam Barlow who was now becoming more and more threatening in his attitude towards the boy.

Then, when Barlow, had heard enough of Steve's appeal to reason, he swore viciously and began to advance on him with his fists clenched and an expression of unmistakable hostility. Steve, himself by now very upset, gave vent to his own bitter frustration by throwing himself at the man when Barlow lunged at him – and here the fact should be brought to light that Steve is a dab hand at karate, having taken lessons in this art of self-defence, although at that time it is not known whether he had reached the standard of proficiency that would have earned him a black belt or brown belt or whatever other distinctions are involved. All the same, he was very good, very quick – and of course Barlow, being the lumbering sort, was always ready with his fists but not versed in activities like karate as Steve was and now set out to prove with dazzling effect so that in a virtual split-second Barlow was lying flat on his back with all the wind knocked out of him.

Sandra was still desperate, she pleaded with her mother not to make her go home – and it seemed for a moment there that Mrs Barlow came up with a solution when, agreeing with Sandra that their home was no longer the place to be, said that she, too, had had enough of the ill-treatment that was to be had there and suggested that the two of them pack some things and clear out while they had the opportunity. Naturally, Sandra was delighted. Yes, of course, that was what they would do; the two of them would leave home together; the future no longer seemed so bleak.

How could Sandra have known then that was just a ruse to get her back in the house, and that her mother had been browbeaten into it? She discovered all too late when she was in her room, hurriedly throwing some clothes into a suitcase and the door was pulled shut and locked from the outside, and she heard the hated voice of the man she had been led to believe was out of the house telling her that she would remain there until she came to her senses.

Before that, as she and her mother had begun to pack for their flight from Summer Bay, Sandra had suddenly thought of Steven and realized how much she would miss him. She couldn't leave without saying goodbye to him, but when she told her mother this, Mrs Barlow had persuaded her to write a farewell note instead which would be easier and free of the complications that could develop from a last meeting or even a telephone call. So Sandra had written a short but tender farewell note, which was delivered to Steve in person by a triumphant Sam Barlow as proof that Sandra and her mother had left town and that there was no longer any point in his bothering his head about the girl.

Steve wasn't convinced, he thought it strange that Sandra would have gone off like that, so suddenly, without telling him anything about what she proposed to do or even hinting at it. But again, with Sandra sitting wretched and hopeless in her locked room, there was nothing he could do except wonder and feel uneasy about the situation.

In all fairness, it might have been Barlow's intention that matters would improve, and possibly he even tried for a while – but what with the drink and everything else, a steady deterioration had set in, and it wasn't long before things were as bad, even worse, than they ever had been. Barlow's mind was clearly going; he was becoming more and more irrational. Finally, during a lull in one particularly violent scene during which many items of household crockery were smashed, Mrs Barlow, obviously having realized by now that there was nothing to be salvaged from this disaster of a marriage after all, quietly and urgently instructed Sandra to fetch Bob Barnett from the police station. She had had enough, she couldn't take any more of it, she was in a state of total exhaustion. She was prepared now to back Sandra in all her complaints against her father. Quietly but desperately, urging her to hurry because Barlow's rage was really murderous this time, she let the girl out through the back door while Barlow continued to rage and break things in the other room.

As it happened, Bob reached the house only just in time, bursting in through the front door to confront

Barlow who was standing over his wife, now slumped in a corner of the living room with blood running down from one side of her mouth onto her chin and the front of her dress. He was just reaching down to grab her when Bob yelled at him to stop. Barlow swung on him. He was out of control now, compelled by the fury that had possessed him and now wouldn't allow him to heed anyone, not even Bob Barnett who represented law and order in the town. He flung himself at Bob who, surprised by the savagery of the onslaught, stepped back and stumbled over a chair that had been overturned during the struggle. As he momentarily lost his balance, Barlow dived at him, his outstretched hands clawing for the policeman's throat.

They were both big men, more or less equally matched in strength, but now that scale was tipped somewhat in Barlow's favour by the power of his rage as, locked together in a fierce embrace, they stumbled and lurched from one side of the room to the other, colliding with what little furniture was still standing, and losing their footing against that which was not, and as their scrabbling feet crunched shards of crockery into the carpet beneath them. Then, somehow, in this confused mêlée which didn't last more than a few moments, Barlow had managed to grab Bob's service revolver from its holster. There was a scream as Mrs Barlow ran forward while Bob, seizing Barlow's wrist, tried to force the weapon up and away from him. The breathing of the two men was loud and intense as they strained against each other. There was a shot, and Mrs Barlow screamed again.

It was a tragic business. Poor Mrs Barlow – all that could be said of her was that she was now at peace, which was fairly much the gist of the sermon that was delivered at her funeral attended by a large number of the townspeople, while Barlow himself, having been denied bail, was awaiting his trial in a city prison where he had plenty of time to regret the error of his ways. It was a fine, sunny day for the funeral. The grave was massed with flowers, and people huddled together in small, subdued groups while a warm, salt-laden breeze wafted in from the ocean. Yes, it was very sad; it had all been so unnecessary.

Until a permanent place could be found for her with a suitable family who could give her the love and care she deserved, Sandra stayed with Ailsa Hogan in her house behind the supermarket. She was still shaken up by what had happened, it would take a long time before she got over it, if she ever did. In the meantime, there was Steve to help her pick up the pieces – and Ailsa, too, of course, who knew exactly what the poor kid had gone through and, in fact, had been stirred by the same hurtful memories that had been aroused by Roo Stewart when she announced in malicious triumph, during the engagement party, that Ailsa, the woman who hoped to marry her father, had once been convicted of murder, although she didn't add, not then being aware of all the details, that Ailsa had been so desperate that she couldn't think of any other way to stop her brutal and drunken father from choking her mother to death that night than by driving the kitchen carving knife into his back with all the strength she could muster.

Four

When the fishing boats come in, the seagulls follow them right to their moorings alongside the fishing co-operative on the other side of the bay from the town. They hover over the craft in a noisy white and scrappy kind of cloud and trail behind them as they return with their catches of the day. Even after the boats are moored and the catch is taken ashore, the birds line up in the hope of pickings and sometimes squabble among themselves, because the seagull can be a very argumentative bird.

The fishing boats come in at roughly the same time every day, and their catch is taken into the co-operative so that we are always assured of fresh fish, although they are not much cheaper than they are in the city markets to where they are despatched in ice.

Another form of fishing is quite popular here, and that is to do it from the beach with a rod and reel in the hope of catching whatever, if anything, is swarming out there beyond the breakers. You see the beach fishermen there at all hours of the day, lined up at the very edge of the sand and staring meditatively out towards the horizon as they wait for a fish to snap up the bait. They're out there at night, too, and if it's chilly they might light a fire to keep them warm. Beach fishing is an activity that demands some dedication.

But for those who are not keen on fishing, there are other ways people can keep themselves occupied. They can run along the beach to keep themselves fit, or they can play bowls or tennis; they can visit our famous National Park where the walking tracks are well signposted so that people won't become lost. Then, of course, for the younger people, there is always the surf; inevitably, whatever the weather, the board-riders wait to pick the right wave that will carry them to the shore in a sweeping and dashing manoeuvre.

There is a sizable proportion of older people in Summer Bay, who have settled on it as an ideal place in which to spend their retirement, where they can fish from the beach, play bowls or walk along the sand in the early morning or late afternoon. While most of these retired people have come here to remain permanently in the warm climate and friendly atmosphere of Summer Bay, there are others who have decided to remain here only as long as it suits them before moving on somewhere else as the mood dictates, in this way seeing the country at their leisure, taking their time because time is something they have in abundance. Yet here again, certain of these nomads, upon lighting on Summer Bay, immediately take a fancy to the place and stay more or less indefinitely but with the idea at the back of their minds that they will travel onwards with their caravan – most of them have caravans which in more recent times have become known as mobile homes – because there is still a great deal more of the country to see.

Floss and Neville McPhee were originally in this latter category of Summer Bay residents. They arrived here some years ago with their caravan to install themselves at the caravan park when it was still owned by Alf Stewart and long before he sold it to Tom and Pippa Fletcher at a reasonable price. Floss and Neville are an elderly couple who have retired from the circus life, which is also a nomadic sort of existence, and probably they had seen enough of the country in any event not to predispose them to seeing it again in a hurry with their caravan – but who knows? They may become restless again one of these days and move on somewhere else.

While she was with the circus, Floss told people's fortunes, and for a while she did the same from her own caravan in Summer Bay until one day she received such a shock when reading what the tarot cards had to say about Bobby Simpson that she put them away there and then and declared that her days as a gypsy fortune-teller were at an end. What she had read in the cards in relation to Bobby Simpson was certainly frightening enough; they hinted that Bobby would be responsible for someone's death, which is one heck of a responsibility to load onto the shoulders of any young girl, even one as tough as Bobby. But now we're jumping ahead a little; Bobby as the harbinger of doom will take her turn in due course. Right now, we are concerned with Floss and Neville and the grandson they had been forbidden to contact or otherwise have any dealings with.

It would seem that any main reason for Floss and Neville remaining in Summer Bay for as long as they have is that while they are here they are still not too far from the city where their son and his wife live in a gracious tree-lined avenue in one of the so-called better suburbs and where their grandson is being reared and taught the finer things of life in total ignorance that his grandparents even existed.

This family estrangement goes back a long way, and

appears to have stemmed from the fact that Scott McPhee is ashamed of his parents because they were circus people, hardly the appropriate background for an ambitious young man who is steadily making his way upward in a profession that might have had something to do with finance or property development, accountancy or even law, any of which noble callings he felt required a fitting background and not one filled with performing seals and gypsy parents and assorted circus freaks, in other words a background filled with the trappings suitable to his station in life, such as a fine two-storey house with a double garage, a swimming pool and all other modern conveniences.

It was only natural that Floss should pine for Ben, the grandson she wasn't allowed to see, natural, too, that she should regard this embargo as being very unfair. She was extremely unhappy about it, to the point that one day she decided to confront her son in the comfortable surroundings of his estate.

It's funny how life is made up of coincidences, as Floss was to declare at a later time, although she did suggest, too, that fate might have had a hand in it, possibly confirming what she might have read in the cards had she done so. But fate or coincidence, what she learnt when she turned up at that grand house in the quiet and leafy boulevard one Saturday morning when she was sure her son and his family would be home was that they were not home and that the woman who opened the door to inform her that the McPhees had just gone away for a week or so was a total stranger to her. Floss wondered if she were the housekeeper, or perhaps a relative from Scott's wife's side of the family. Anyway, she was quite crestfallen at coming all this way from Summer Bay on a mission that proved to be fruitless, and she was just about to turn away when the woman asked her if she had come about the job.

Job? Floss was instantly alert. She was also thinking quickly. She turned back to face the woman who was regarding her steadily from the doorway. Yes, well, as a matter of fact . . . She hedged, having no idea what sort of job the woman was talking about. She nodded her head and tried to look as if she did. The woman sized her up and down with a critical eye, nodded curtly as if satisfied with her examination of the job applicant, then proceeded, unbidden, to tell Floss what her duties would entail if she were to be successful, and from her attitude it seemed to be that she was the one who would be doing the hiring or rejecting, as the case may be. As to the nature of the duties, Floss was delighted to learn that they would be nothing less than acting as a temporary nanny to her own grandson while his parents were away, although, naturally, she concealed her delight, remaining quite impassive and matter-of-fact while the woman talked. But, of course, she was then told, and this made her catch her breath a little and engage in some more quick thinking, personal references would be needed before she could even be considered for the job. Of course, Floss said, nodding keenly; that would be no trouble at all, she told the woman, providing her with the telephone numbers of Ailsa Hogan and Pippa Fletcher both of whom she was positive would back her to the hilt, particularly when they learnt of this ideal opportunity for Floss to get to know her grandson in a situation free of parental disapproval. Even if she couldn't get through to them first and warn them that they would be approached, she was sure they would come up with the goods. Like herself, they were quick thinkers.

And so it proved. Floss got the job which made her happy, and Neville, who'd had his reservations about Floss's intention to confront the younger McPhees in the first place, unhappy. When she told him about the job, he objected most strongly. She was asking for trouble, he insisted; all she could expect for her pains was a kick in the teeth, which would serve her right. But Floss didn't see it that way, and they had quite an argument about it until finally Neville grumbled that he was washing his hands of the whole affair.

To Floss's disappointment, little Ben, her grandson, didn't turn out to be quite the charmer she had fondly imagined, with a distant smile. He was sullen and uncommunicative; he was defiant and unco-operative, and seemed to have taken an instant dislike to the woman he believed was the nanny who had been hired to look after him while his parents were away. He did everything he could to antagonize her, and Floss soon found herself drawing deeply on her reserves of patience, telling herself it was only because the boy was spoilt that he was behaving in such an offensive manner. He had obviously been given everything he wanted even if he didn't deserve it. A good sharp slap Floss thought, would have been the order of the day. So, ever hopeful that she would eventually get through to the kid with a little kindness and understanding, Floss persevered in this fine house where everything was exactly in place, polished and spotless, and which didn't have a lived-in look about it at all.

However, she soon discovered that her reserves of patience were not limitless, and she lashed sharply out at him when he plucked the photograph album she was dreamily browsing through from her hands because he said it was none of her business. It was then that she did slap him. Giving her a startled look, his eyes already brimming with tears, he dropped the album and darted across to the telephone to where the woman who had interviewed Floss had left the number on which Ben's parents could be contacted in case of emergency. Snuffling and sniffling, knuckling the tears from his eyes with his free hand, the boy began to dial the number while Floss placidly watched him from the other side of the room.

She listened to him as he tearfully pleaded with his father to come home because he was missing him – and his mother, too – and this woman who was here to look after him while they were away, well she wasn't at all nice . . . He shot his grandmother a defiant look, then held out the receiver to her with the muttered information that his father wanted to talk to her. Floss was suddenly nervous; she hadn't spoken to her son for years, but she was apprehensive that he would recognize her voice nevertheless, even on the telephone, and challenge her, demanding to know what sort of deceitful game she was playing. But with her grandson shrewdly eyeing her, she had no choice but to take the receiver he was holding out to her, and lowering her voice an octave or two, hope for the best.

To her relief, Scott didn't recognize her voice; in fact, he sounded quite pleasant and surprised her somewhat by telling her she had a free hand as far as the boy was concerned, meaning she shouldn't allow him to get away with murder which was what he would do if she didn't put a stop to that sort of nonsense right away, and in

44

no uncertain terms. Floss agreed with him that that was the best way, and smiled across at the boy, whose turn it now was to look a little apprehensive.

She gradually got through to him; all it took was a little kindness and interest in him, and although he was still wary at first, he slowly began to respond and go some way towards proving himself to be the small boy Floss had often imagined him to be.

When she mentioned her idea of bringing Ben up to Summer Bay for a few days to Neville, who had just driven down to the city to see how she was faring with her charge, he was appalled. No, it wouldn't do, he said firmly; he absolutely forbade it and urged her to banish such a crazy notion from her head because it would only mean trouble and disaster. But Floss was determined to see that her grandson was exposed to the sunshine and fresh air that is Summer Bay's stock-in-trade, and accused Neville of being a nervous nellie, quite afraid of his own shadow. Ben was coming to Summer Bay for a few days and that was that, absolutely final, so no more argument please.

It was a simple matter to get Scott to agree that his son could accompany the temporary nanny to Summer Bay for a couple of days. The fresh air and sunshine would be good for him, Scott acknowledged when his mother suggested this in a voice that was once again slightly deeper than normal. A splendid idea, he said, becoming more and more enthusiastic about the proposal. So, much to the misgivings of Neville, who still foresaw doom and destruction even though he had made no career of fortune-telling as had his wife who didn't seem in the least concerned, it was arranged.

As Floss had predicted, even without cards or other

implements of the trade, young Ben took to the fresh air and sunshine of Summer Bay very well indeed. He loved the beach and the sand and the rolling surf, and found a friend in Sally, the youngest of the Fletcher foster-children. In spite of himself Neville was quite touched to see them playing together, totally absorbed in what they were doing, although this had no effect on his impatience with the boy while they were having dinner in the caravan since Ben's table manners left quite a lot to be desired, when he blurted out without thinking that the boy was as bad as his father when he was the same age. Floss gave him a sharp and reproachful look, and they both looked at the boy to see what his reaction was to this statement, but Ben was quite intent on carving up his pork chop and appeared to be unaware of the gaffe just committed by his grandfather.

The following afternoon, Floss and Neville returned from their customary walk along the beach to find Ben, who had elected not to come with them, sitting on the floor of the caravan surrounded by odds and ends he had extracted from Floss's old tin chest which he had been rummaging through, and scattering on the floor around him. As they stomped up the steps into the caravan, he looked up at them suspiciously, then held up one of the photographs which Floss kept in the chest. 'Hey,' he demanded, 'how come you got pictures of my father?' Floss and Neville stared at him; it was time for some more quick thinking.

There were quite a number of pictures of Scott as a boy and a young man before he had become successful and his hair had turned slightly grey at the edges in Floss's old tin trunk. It hadn't occurred to Floss that in the spirit of youthful exploration Ben would unearth them during the time he had been left alone in the caravan. With a quick and apprehensive glance at Neville, she began to explain to Ben that those photographs were not of his father but someone who bore a striking resemblance to him – a coincidence, she said, that was quite amazing, but such coincidences did happen and perhaps were not as uncommon as was generally supposed. But Ben wasn't taken in by this; those photographs were definitely of his father who he knew back to front; there was no mistaking that it was his father; he had made up his mind about that and his mind couldn't be changed.

In the end, Floss had to stop arguing because the boy was being so adamant about those snapshots he said were of his father, picking up one of them after the other and displaying them as undeniable proof of the fact. All right, all right, she conceded at last with a helpless shrug at Neville whose expression confirmed all his earlier dire and doom-laden predictions of what would come of his wife's folly, the pictures were of his father as a boy and young man. But why? Ben demanded, returning to his original question. Because he is our son, Floss told him unhappily, then added while the boy was still digesting this revelation, that she and Neville were his grandparents, something Ben flatly refused to believe until she produced documentary evidence that proved the fact, and even then he remained sceptical. Then, after a while, as it dawned on him that these people were actually who they said they were, he began to feel betrayed. He had been tricked; it had been a mean thing for them to do, pretending like that to be someone they were not when they were in fact his grandparents. By now, Floss herself was quite upset as she tried to explain that the only reason they had deceived was in the hope of getting to know him better, but now that they had been found out there was nothing else for it but to take him back to the city.

As he listened to his grandmother and realized how sad she was at the failure of her plan, Ben became quite affected himself. He was no longer bitter; his eyes were moist, his lips were trembling a little. No, he cried; he didn't want to go back to the city, he was having such a nice time up here on the beach where he had found friends to play with – and, anyway, if he had suddenly found himself loaded with a pair of unexpected grand-parents, he was glad that they were Neville and Floss who were so kind to him and who were so liked by everyone he had met up here in Summer Bay. Anyway, that was the gist of his meaning if not his actual words.

He wanted to stay with them in Summer Bay, and Floss was exceptionally happy about that. Even Neville was happy despite the reservations he still harboured, because he had developed quite a liking for the boy. Everyone was happy; they began to devise plans for the remainder of Ben's stay, beginning with a picnic in the National Park the following day if the weather was fine.

They were getting along famously. Neville took his grandson prospecting along the beach with a metal detector – something else to do in Summer Bay – and they were both gratified when they unearthed someone's wristwatch that had probably been lost at the height of the previous season when there were so many strangers about. They went for walks together and watched the board-riders shooting the waves. When it was time for him to be taken back to the city, Ben said he didn't want to go because he had never been as happy in the city as he had been these past couple of days at Summer Bay. He wanted to stay with his new-found grandparents and his new-found friends; he wouldn't miss his school, or even his parents who were always so busy and never seemed to have much time for him in any event.

As much as they would have liked him to stay, Floss and Neville realized that this was impossible; he would have to return to his school and his parents, but that didn't mean he would stop seeing his grandparents at Summer Bay, even after his parents returned from their holiday – Neville, in particular, was most determined about that, having experienced a tremendous softening of his heart towards the boy, just as he was determined to do everything in his power to ensure that he and Floss would have continued access to their grandson. If possible, he was even more iron-willed about this by now than Floss was, and even suggested that she consult her tarot cards or look into her crystal ball to see how the business would end. In the meantime, it was arranged that Ben should also spend the following weekend with them in their caravan, which mollified his feelings to a large extent.

It was a long week for Neville while Floss and Ben were away in the city; he missed them both terribly. But finally it was time for him to drive down and collect them. When he saw his grandfather, Ben rushed into his arms and hardly stopped talking all the way back to Summer Bay, he was so excited to be going there again.

Of course, it couldn't have lasted forever; the show-down would have had to come sooner or later; it was only to be expected that calamity would descend on them sooner or later – and when it turned in through the entrance to the caravan park later that afternoon Neville was the first to recognize it.

Calamity, in this instance, took the form of a dark Mercedes-Benz motor car which contained the personages of the younger Mr and Mrs McPhee, who having cut short their holiday, had stopped by at Summer Bay on their way home to reclaim their son from the well-intentioned nanny who had been hired to look after him during their absence and for two weekends in succession had been giving him a treat by taking him to her caravan on the beach. Yet again, it was time for some quick thinking to be done.

But this time there was no way out of it; the music had to be faced; the identity of the nanny had to be revealed and the unpleasantness that would result from that endured. Telling Ben to remain in the caravan, Floss and Neville stepped out of the caravan and moved across to the car beside which their son Scott was standing with a perplexed expression as he stared around the site for a glimpse of his son. This perplexity clouded over into anger when he saw who was approaching him, and putting two and two together, realized that he had been tricked.

Oh, it was a fine old barney that took place then among the caravans. Scott, shouting at his parents and red in the face, actually accused them of kidnapping his son. He called them all sorts of names. Floss, managing to get a word in, stemmed this tirade only long enough to give an impassioned explanation of her motives which were, simply, the desire to re-establish contact with her son, long-estranged, and when the opportunity to get to know her grandson had come her way in a manner that even she could not have predicted she had seized it as any grandmother would have done under similar circumstances. But Scott wasn't having any of that; he refused to listen to her. He shouted and raged, and while a small knot of interested spectators gathered to witness the proceedings, bounded across to the caravan, wrenched open the door, disappeared and a moment later re-emerged with young Ben who was howling and protesting that he didn't want to go home. Floss and Neville could only stand by and watch miserably as the wailing boy was thrust by his legal parent into the motor car where his mother took him in her arms and unsuccessfully tried to console him.

Scott had a few more choice remarks to deliver to his hapless parents while the gathering crowd looked on with interest. He shouted and gesticulated a lot; he fumed and foamed. Desperately, Floss broke in again to demand what it was that made them such social outcasts in his eyes, but all he did by way of reply was point contemptuously to the caravan in which they had decided to spend their days and which, it probably should have been said earlier, is in a remarkably dilapidated condition. A few moments later, the younger McPhees had sped off with their restored offspring in their expensive car which raised a cloud of dust as it went and almost clipped one of the gateposts at the entrance to the caravan park.

The next move made by Floss and Neville was more in the nature of a rearguard action, a desperate move that didn't achieve much more than considerable embarrassment to their son and his wife whose neighbours didn't take too kindly to the majestic appearance of their street being marred by an old and dilapidated caravan which parked conspicuously outside the McPhee's residence, or to the old woman with the scarf knotted around her head who offered to tell their fortunes. But for that while it was a stand-off between the older and younger McPhees who resolutely refused to discuss the matter when this was made a condition for the removal of the caravan and the gypsy fortune-teller who was harrassing the neighbours. Floss and Neville refused to budge unless Scott talked. Scott just refused to talk, and threatened to call the police, and Ben was kept inside the house.

When the police car did pull up in front of the house, Floss and Neville naturally thought that Scott had made good his threat and called them, but as it transpired it wasn't Scott who had summoned them but Ben who had formulated some sort of strange idea of making a complaint against his parents for cruelty or something similar, so that he would then be allowed to return to Summer Bay with his grandparents. When they learned this, and after some discussion with the police sergeant, who sympathized with their position but nevertheless had his duty to perform, both Floss and Neville sadly realized that matters had gotten quite out of hand and that there was nothing else for it but to beat a dignified retreat back to Summer Bay to lick their wounds.

As they were preparing to leave, Ben suddenly called to them in a voice of desperation from one of the upstairs windows. 'Hey!' he cried. 'Don't go! Take me with you!'

But they couldn't take him with them, enough damage had already been done, and it was for his own good that they quietly left and picked up the threads of life again in the Summer Bay caravan park. It was hard – very hard, but they had to do it to ensure that the boy's relationship with his father was not permanently damaged, which would be a terrible thing. So they forced themselves.

Floss choked back her sobs, and there was a slight waver in Neville's voice as he gruffly called back up to the small boy in the upstairs window. 'You've caused us nothing but trouble,' he said with a firm shake of his head as he blinked away the tears that stung his eyes. 'We don't want to see you any more.'

They drove away quickly and didn't once look back.

Five

When it was decided that what Celia Stewart really needed was a man – a good, solid, down-to-earth type who wouldn't put up with any of her nonsense and who would snap her out of her silly, scatterbrained ways and that the lack of any male influence was probably what was basically wrong with her – the obvious choice in the eyes of Ailsa Hogan and Celia's brother, Alf, was Bob Barnett, the town policeman and a man of firmness and commonsense. Added to that was that he was a man of reasonable looks and physique, but more importantly was unattached. It was towards this end of bringing them more closely together that they invited them both to Ailsa's place for dinner one night.

Because Celia was a very unrelaxed sort of woman, it was Alf's idea to ply her with a sufficient quantity of liquor beforehand so that she would be more suitably relaxed in the policeman's company – a good idea as far as it went, but the liquid refreshment went even further than was intended and Celia, usually so sparing as far as such beverages were concerned, ended up by becoming quite whoopsy. She became shrill and giggly, and laughed uproariously at the most unexpected places in the conversation – and finally, Alf's whispered prediction to Ailsa that his sister would be in Bob's arms before the evening was out proved literally true as they thoughtfully watched him carry her out of the house in his arms to drive her home and put her to bed where she could continue her sleep in greater comfort.

If matters had taken their course, and Bob and Celia had taken more than a passing interest in each other, they probably would have gone on seeing each other and may have eventually become engaged as their benefactors, Alf and Ailsa, had recently done. In time, perhaps, they would have become married and set about the business of starting a family if it was in their minds to do so – all perfectly ordinary and straightforward, and perfectly pleasing to Alf and Ailsa who had brought them together in the first place.

Roo Stewart, Alf's daughter, on the other hand, ambled along this path in the opposite direction. First she got herself pregnant, then decided she needed a father for this forthcoming happy event. The next item on the agenda would be marriage to make it all above board.

The actual father – or would-be father – of Roo's child was a fellow called Brett something with whom she had become involved in the city, where she had gone after a blazing row with her father over his proposed marriage to Ailsa Hogan, an action she regarded as a betrayal and which she had tried to forestall; she failed dismally, by introducing during the engagement party the two of them had arranged for the friends and neighbours a sensational element regarding Ailsa's past life. She had run away from home and in the city had met this boy Brett, and nature had simply taken its course. When he learned about Roo's condition Brett had offered to foot the bill to have the pregnancy terminated, but was prepared to go no further than that, having an eye to future prospects which didn't call for him to tie himself down at such a young age. But as he said, he thought he was doing the right and proper thing by offering to pay the necessary expenses which was by no means what every other young man in the same situation would do. He left the choice open to her.

When Roo, feeling anxious and vulnerable, and realizing how badly she was in need of paternal support in this time of crisis, turned up back in Summer Bay, Alf was naturally pleased to see her but was, at the same time, a little suspicious about what amounted to her sudden change of heart in relation to Ailsa whom she now said she was prepared to accept as her stepmother, having had plenty of time while she was in the city to think the matter over thoroughly. She even went so far as to apologize for her outburst. Of course, she made no mention of what she was bringing back from the city with her; that would have to remain a secret for as long as it was possible, by which time she hoped to have matters arranged in a way that was quite satisfactory to all.

If Alf's doubts were allayed by his daughter's sincerity and apologetic demeanour, this was certainly not the case with Ailsa who, knowing the girl as well as she did, was quite convinced that if she were not already up to some more mischief designed to drive a wedge between Alf and herself, she very soon would be. But when Roo managed to get her alone for a few minutes, she agreed that an antagonism still existed between them but declared that she really didn't want to make waves, and for her father's sake wished to establish an atmosphere of outward harmony at least in the household. Ailsa had no choice but to go along with her. All the same, she remained very watchful.

The next thing Roo did was make up with Frank, the oldest of the Fletcher foster-brood with whom there had been an attachment in the past, but this, too, had been disrupted by a quarrel on the eve of Roo's flight to the city. Now, finding him at work in her father's liquor store, she was all sweetness and light, butter not melting in her mouth, as she explained to him that there really was a fine line between love and hate, and if what she had said to him at the height of their argument had sounded hateful it wasn't because she hated him – oh no, the words had just come out that way as they tended to do in such quarrels – but because she loved him and that it had really been an expression of the frustration she felt in not thinking at the time that her love for him was being returned in full. By now Frank was totally confused, but agreed, for the sake of preventing another argument, that it made some sort of sense. Roo gave him one of her dazzling smiles and said, there, she knew he would understand, she was still very fond of him – no, more than that, her feelings for him hadn't changed in the slightest. Frank found himself gradually being won over by her persuasiveness. Whatever hard feelings that might have existed when she sought him out in the liquor store had softened to a subsistency reasonably close to mush.

Having established that much, Roo's aim was to entice Frank into a situation in which they would consummate their feelings for each other in such a way as to provide justification for the event that would inevitably occur some months later, and was a classic example of how crafty she could be when she set her mind to it. Poor Frank, besotted as he was, was completely ignorant of the role she had elected for him to play in her little drama – but even so, when she suggested to him, rather breathlessly and with the carefully illuminated light of love shining in her eyes, that they make that aforementioned commitment to their feelings for each other, Frank showed some initial reluctance. It was too premature, he said with a little difficulty; too hasty; they had to be absolutely sure they were doing the right thing . . . 'But Frank,' she returned with husky fervour as her fingers lightly touched his arm and she brought forth all her impressive armoury of seductive wiles so that Frank found it increasingly impossible to resist, 'Frank, it's us, the two of us, it *would* be the right thing.' And so on in this vein, until Frank found the invitation impossible to resist, the last of his reservations having flown out the window. Later, when she whispered to him, 'Please be careful, Frank, because you're the first,' the infamy of this little minx was compounded.

Perhaps Roo did have twinges of conscience after all about what she had set out to do; perhaps, too, she was beginning to realize that her feelings for Frank were more genuine than she had thought when she started out on her hard-hearted little game, but when Alf Stewart discovered Frank leaving Roo's room one night, he came to an immediate, and outraged conclusion, and not only sacked him from his job in the liquor store but ordered him to stay away from his daughter who he had relied on Frank to respect and leave alone in his absence, Roo began to have qualms that were not before time in arriving. She found herself genuinely very sorry for what had happened.

Now the suspicion was that Roo had deliberately engineered it so that she and Frank would actually be discovered in a compromising position by Alf when he returned home that evening. In Alf's eyes, in any event, this would have been the clincher in the matter of Frank's soon-to-be paternity status. If this was right, she probably told Frank that her father wouldn't be coming home until some time later than she knew he really was, which would have served to allay Frank's worries about possible discovery– worries, incidentally, that had proved to be justified when Alf discovered Frank on the landing outside his daughter's door with an expression that told him all and made him blow his top. Again, if this suspicion is correct, Roo must have been holding her breath as she strained to hear the arrival of her father in the house which, on this occasion, might have come a fraction too late.

If Roo had foreseen that her father wouldn't be too pleased with the young man who had betrayed his trust, she obviously didn't expect that his displeasure would extend to his firing Frank from his job in the liquor store which made a much-needed financial contribution to the Fletcher household whose resources were strained enough as it was. Nor, perhaps, could she have anticipated that her father would ban the two of them from seeing each other again, which wasn't what she had in mind at all, and which was no easy accomplishment in a town as small as Summer Bay. Frank, for his part, was less put out by the loss of his job than by the fact that he was forbidden to see Roo again.

After Frank's banishment from the house, Alf Stewart lectured his daughter very severely on the pitfalls of giving way to one's momentary passions. What if she found herself pregnant as a result of this little escapade? What indeed? Roo looked suitably chastened.

The general feeling was that Frank was best out of it,

that there was no future for him with a girl like Ruth Stewart – and probably no one was more pleased about this than Bobby Simpson who had been getting along very nicely with Frank before Roo came back on the scene, and who, when Frank told her of his misfortunes, graciously resisted the urge to gloat and say, 'I told you so.' Ailsa Hogan, too, was pleased that Frank had been ordered to stay away from Roo who she was convinced was still up to no good no matter what assurances she might have made, but at the same time was appalled that Frank should have been sacked because of his involvement with the girl. When she confronted Alf and demanded to know what was happening, he flatly refused to discuss it, which she could hardly think was a favourable beginning if they intended to spend the rest of their lives together. They had quite a row about it, she accused him of being bull-headed and unfair, of mixing business with personal considerations, and Alf told her not to meddle in something that didn't concern her, at which Ailsa laughed harshly and without a trace of humour at the ridiculous proposal that she shouldn't voice an opinion on something that was crucial to their future happiness together – and there the matter remained for the time being except that Ailsa angered Alf even more by offering Frank a job in her supermarket, which the boy eagerly accepted, and to which Alf reacted, after another heated exchange of words and sentiments, by breaking off the engagement. Naturally, this outcome at least was gratifying to Roo.

Roo and Frank might have been banned from seeing each other, but that didn't mean they couldn't find ways and means of circumventing that ban whenever they could do so without the possibility of being observed, in which activity they showed quite some resourcefulness. In the meantime, deciding she needed an ally, Roo chose her Aunt Celia as being the most suitable candidate and the one most likely to keep her silence about Roo's pregnancy for fear of family shame and scandal, a worry that was always uppermost in her aunt's mind and which had been given a bad jolt that night at Ailsa's when she had made such a spectacle of herself in front of Bob Barnett, the town policeman. Playing on this fear of Celia's, and after the shock of the revelation that she was pregnant had subsided a little, Roo managed to convince her that they should work together to bring Alf round to the idea that Frank wasn't nearly so bad as he thought. With his blessing – or even just his lack of opposition – Roo and Frank could then be married and the baby brought up in the protective shade of respectability without anyone being any the wiser about the truth of the matter. Celia had no choice but to agree that respectability for the baby should be the major consideration.

With her aunt now on her side, Roo decided that the next thing to do was let Frank in on the secret, and left it to Celia to break the news to the father-elect. Frank's reaction to the news, when she presented it to him, was a pleased one and he couldn't see any reason for the secrecy that was now being urged on him by Roo. But Roo was most insistent about that, leaving Frank with no choice but to go along with the scheme.

They had to pick their time to inform Alf of their intention to get married; he had to be in a good mood and receptive to the idea. But when Roo picked the time for her and Frank to break the news of their wedding plans to her father, that good mood quickly disappeared to be replaced by a very angry one indeed. He was furious, and ordered Frank to leave his house, while banishing Roo to her room. Celia tried to make him see that the young couple had set their hearts on becoming husband and wife because they loved each other – and what better reason could there be than that? she added a little wistfully before returning to the attack on her brother who was being so obdurate. But the more unreasonable she accused him of being, the more Alf suspected a plot and refused to be budged.

Frank had already announced his intentions to Tom and Pippa Fletcher, his foster parents, with regard to Roo, neatly fielding the expected question from Tom by replying, no, he didn't have to marry her, it wasn't like that at all. Thus reassured, Tom and Pippa had wished him luck and had said they would keep their fingers crossed for him. Now he was back again, with Roo, who had climbed out of her bedroom window to join him in the garden below. The two of them decided then that if they were to get any further with their plans they should get Tom and Pippa onto their side. But while Roo was talking to Pippa in one part of the house, woman to woman, and insisting that she and Frank wished to marry only for love, Frank was having a more rocky time of it in another part of the house where he and Tom were talking man to man.

Tom was sceptical. While he had earlier accepted Frank's denial that there was a compelling need for him to marry Roo Stewart, it seemed that there was something in the boy's attitude, perhaps in the over-confident way in which he expressed himself, that made him once more suspicious that certain salient facts were being kept from him – or one salient fact in particular. He didn't beat about the bush, which was never Tom's style. He pressed and dug; he chipped away – and finally Frank was unable to keep it back any longer; he admitted the truth of what his foster father suspected; yes, Roo was expecting a baby; yes, he was the father. It came as something of a relief to get it out in the open at last.

So the secret was out, it was no longer a secret. Tom decided that the best thing the four of them could do now would be to form a deputation to approach Alf with the news that there was, after all, a definite need for Roo and Frank to get married other than for reasons of love and romance.

It stood to reason that Alf would be stunned by the news that what he had warned Roo against had actually come to pass. It stood to reason too that he needed some time to think about it in order to come to terms with this surprise development, and once he had done that to realize that it could have been worse, that the father could have been someone completely unknown to him, perhaps with characteristics that were less desirable than those to be found in Frank, after that he would give his blessing no doubt to the marriage. It stood to reason that Frank and Roo would be made ecstatic by this consent so gruffly given by Roo's father. Now, that had been achieved, the plans could go ahead for the wedding.

It might have proceeded from there smoothly enough provided Frank had greater success than he was having in his hunt for a job which would bring in a greater income than his part-time employment at Ailsa Hogan's supermarket, and which, with his new and sudden responsibilities, would enable them to move into something better than the caravan that would have to do for a start until an improvement in their situation could be guaranteed – it might have been plain sailing, more or less, if Bobby Simpson, whose feelings for Frank still gave her a vested interest in his future, hadn't smelt a rat, and resolved to expose Roo for the manipulative creature she knew her to be.

As Ailsa told her, the evidence on which she based her suspicions was both flimsy and dangerous – but Bobby didn't see it that way at all. She had overheard the exchange between Roo and Frank when Roo inadvertently let out the fact that the baby had just kicked, and Frank, with some knowledge about these things, certainly as they affected Pippa's pregnancy – still ongoing with no complications as yet – had said in some puzzlement that the baby couldn't be kicking yet, it was too early for it to be so active. While Roo quickly covered her tracks by saying yes, of course, he was right, she must have just imagined it, anticipated what was still to come, Bobby had nevertheless made some rapid calculations in her head based on the premise that the baby *had* kicked, this being hardly the sort of thing she would conjure up just to keep the conversation flowing, and came to the conclusion that it was much too early for the infant to be kicking if it had been conceived after Roo's return to Summer Bay, which Frank was absolutely positive about. To make sure about this Bobby brought up the subject with him in a roundabout sort of way so as not to make him unduly suspicious. That was when she decided to expose Roo for the schemer she was, and by doing so leave the field open for a renewed relationship with Frank who, in a dream she still vividly recalled, had kissed her at the church altar after they had been proclaimed man and wife, and there had been flowers everywhere.

She made no secret to Roo that she proposed to bring her unstuck, which rattled that girl severely now that she was within sight of her goal and could see, thanks to Bobby, all her carefully laid out plans coming to nothing if she didn't do something about it. While she was left to contemplate this awkward development, Bobby set out to put the necessary mechanisms in motion to make good her threat.

When she learned, employing the roundabout methods at which she was becoming so adept, from Carly Morris, Roo's friend, that Roo had mentioned once or twice a boy she had met in the city whose name was Brett something, Roo hadn't mentioned his last name, or if she had Carly had forgotten what it was, instinct told Bobby, bingo, this Brett something was the most likely culprit.

On the trail, Bobby's next move was to raid Roo's school locker in the hope of unearthing something that would take her a step further – and again, bingo, she was lucky; she not only came up with the name of this Brett, by hurriedly leafing through an address book she found in the locker, but his address in the city, to where she hurried at the first available opportunity – and here yet another piece fell into place as, pretending to be Roo's best friend and confidant, she tricked him into admitting his paternity of Roo's child. But at this point Bobby's luck ran out when Brett flatly refused to involve himself any further by telling Frank what he had just admitted to Bobby. He had given Roo her chance; now he was washing his hands of the whole affair. Bobby tried, pointing out what his admission would mean to Frank who would otherwise be trapped into a marriage which Bobby knew in her heart was destined for disaster, but Brett refused to be budged in the matter. Defeated, Bobby returned unhappily to Summer Bay where she decided to take the bull by the horns and confront Frank with what she had discovered so far.

But Frank was in no mood to listen to her. Roo had already anticipated Bobby by telling him that Bobby meant trouble, had threatened to make trouble in any way she could, and otherwise turned Frank's feelings against the girl, who was only trying to save him from being used so despicably. So when Bobby did confront him and began to tell him what she knew, Frank, fore-warned, lost his temper with her and ordered her from his caravan. Bobby was very cut-up about having so alienated the young man she loved, and could see Roo's fine hand behind this abrupt change in him.

That was how the matter stood, with the baby steadily growing and taking shape inside the expectant mother and bride-to-be, when who should turn up out of the blue but the part-creator of this budding life who had since had plenty of time to consider the position while recovering from a bout of the mumps.

It was the mumps that had done it, he explained to Roo who, on being told by her Aunt Celia that a young man called Brett had come to see her while she was out, had gone down to the beach where he had said he would be and found him sitting on a sand dune. The mumps which had come upon him so unexpectedly had had an unfortunate side effect not unusual with such ailment. The mumps, he said dolefully as he stared out at the point around which the fishing boats were coming with their attendant flock of seagulls, had made him sterile, which meant, he went on, that the baby Roo was carrying was the only one he would ever father, hence the reason for his change of heart in wanting to claim the baby after all.

Roo was both angry and incredulous at hearing this. It was too late for that now, she said; her plans had been made, and she couldn't be expected to hand over her baby to him, just like that, as soon as it was born. No, she stated with resolute firmness, she would not give up the baby, *her* baby, to him just because he had recently recovered from a bout of the mumps.

But Brett was just as determined as she was. Okay then, he said just as firmly, if she didn't hand over the baby he would tell Frank of the circumstances surrounding its conception, which wouldn't please Frank at all and would undoubtedly put paid to her wedding plans. To which Roo had her own threat to make; if Brett did as he threatened and interfered with those wedding plans, she would take certain steps to have that budding life terminated, something of a bluff because the baby was already kicking, as Bobby had overheard her say, and Roo was in no way certain what the medical ramifications would be if she took the steps she had threatened. However, she did have a proposal to make; if Brett didn't make any trouble she promised she would find a way to deliver the baby to him at some time in the future when the relationship with Frank had grown and stabilized to the point where it could stand alone – a rash promise to be sure, Frank's feelings towards the disposal of the baby he believed to be his were not taken into consideration, but such details were overlooked in Roo's desperation to get Brett off her back. In any case, Brett thought about this proposition for a few moments while gazing out at the fishing boats before finally nodding his acceptance.

Now enters Morag, sister of Celia and Alf, and aunt

of Roo who she was firmly convinced was marrying beneath her station, Morag being a lady of quality and highly placed in the legal profession, and whose dismay at the news of the forthcoming nuptials had brought her hurrying to Summer Bay. She worked on Roo, tried hard to dissuade her from such folly as marrying Frank who she didn't think had much going for him in the way of prospects. She could do much better for herself, Aunt Morag insisted, it was simply madness to throw away her life like that. But Roo was just as insistent; she loved Frank and intended to marry him, no matter what his prospects which, she was sure, would pick up in any event. She stood her ground, and Morag, for once, was unable to influence the course of events – or so she thought.

It was Celia, chatting away non-stop as usual, who made Morag aware of the existence of a young man called Brett something who had come to see Roo while she was out and who apparently must have made mention of the fact that he was staying in one of the local motels for a couple of days or so, because that was where Morag, recalling something else Celia had told her with regard to a scandalous suggestion of Bobby Simpson's that Frank was not the father of Roo's baby, tracked him down and set to work to extract the truth of what she already suspected of him, a task that was somewhat easier for her when she discovered that she knew this young man and his family, who were also highly respectable. By one means or another, she did manage to get him to confirm her suspicions. Yes, he admitted quite freely; he was the father of Roo's baby.

Armed with this information, a grim-faced Morag then confronted her errant niece and warned her, most severely, that a marriage based on falsehood would only end in disaster. To Roo's growing consternation, she revealed that she knew the whole story but quickly went on to reassure her that she wouldn't give her away. All the same, she was most concerned for her niece's future; she begged Roo to think the matter over very carefully before committing herself to this irrevocable step which would only end in misery.

But Roo didn't need to think; her mind was already made up. Her aunt was being unduly pessimistic, she thought. Of course it would work out all right. She would make sure it would. In the meantime, the wedding day drew closer; preparations were made in a flurry, details were overlooked, and then remembered at the last minute – and in the midst of all this scurrying back and forth, Floss McPhee's dreams, also overlooked in the excitement, loomed large and threatening.

Six

Floss's dream was very vivid, down to the last detail; it frightened the life out of her. She had jerked awake with a palpitating heart and the echo of a startled cry dying on her lips. She gasped and looked across at Neville who had also been jolted awake by Floss's cry and the sudden movement as she sat bolt upright in the bed and tried to catch her breath. 'I've seen it,' she whispered in a doom-laden voice. 'I know whose death Bobby is going to cause.'

It had been an awful revelation that had come to her in her sleep. She had seen the car, a white car, now nothing more than mangled and crumpled metal; she could even recall its licence number. She had seen the body lying inert in the wreckage. 'My God,' she whispered again in the same doomstruck tone. 'It's Frank.'

Neville told her it was nonsense, superstitious hysteria, it was just a dream, that was all it was, and in any case, the Fletchers didn't own a white car, which should be proof enough that Floss's dream didn't mean anything. But Floss refused to be pacified; she placed great store on her dreams many of which had come true, although none of those had foretold such a tragic and alarming event. She was very frightened, the dream had been so vivid, and it confirmed what she had already seen in the tarot cards. Oh yes, it had told her as clearly as anything could tell her that Bobby Simpson would be responsible for Frank's sudden death.

Having been forbidden by Neville to mention her dream to either Bobby or Frank for fear of making herself look ridiculous, Floss was left to carry the burden of it on her own shoulders, but not without a fiercely intense struggle with her conscience. Perhaps Neville was right, she tried to tell herself without too much conviction, and it signified nothing after all. As he had pointed out to her, the Fletchers didn't even have a white car with the licence number she remembered so clearly.

Then, suddenly, to her complete and utter horror, she did see the car again, and this time it wasn't in a dream, it was very real and so close to her that she could almost have reached out and touched it. When she saw it turn into the caravan park that afternoon, and recognized it down to the last detail as it had appeared in her dream, even to the licence number; when she saw Frank behind the wheel of this white car of her dream, she paled and felt quite faint so that she had to grasp the door of the caravan to prevent herself from falling.

What she hadn't known at the time of her dream – what no one had known because Frank had meant it to be a surprise – was that he had been putting some money aside to buy himself a second-hand car. This he had just done the day Floss saw him driving into the caravan park. While it might have been a surprise for everyone else who had an interest in the matter, it had come as a shock of the most unpleasant sort to Floss, who, apart from her other fortune-telling abilities, could apparently dream into the future – and if this much of it had come true, then that meant . . . She shuddered and passed a hand over her face as if to wipe away the vision. She closed her eyes firmly, then opened them again – but the car with Frank now climbing out of it with a broad grin was still there.

When she told Neville of what she had seen, then showed him the car which was parked outside the Fletcher house, he blinked a few times, looked slightly abashed and forced himself to admit that his wife's dream had certainly been remarkable, especially now that the details of it borne out in real life. Most remarkable, he said as he thoughtfully massaged his jaw, then told her to do what she thought best under the circumstances.

Floss's first action on receiving this husbandly approval was to seek out Bobby in whom Floss's original prediction that she would one day be responsible for someone's death had continued to niggle. When Floss told her about her dream, Bobby, too, looked thoughtful and reassured her that she intended to steer well clear of Frank, the potential victim. Floss's relief at hearing this was short-lived, however; when, despite Bobby's reassurances, she later saw the girl who, as it turned out had reluctantly, and after much persuasion on the part of Frank to show off his new car, gone for a ride in that vehicle which, with both of them on board, was now pulling into the car park, she panicked and while Frank rushed into his house to pick up a couple of beach towels because they had arranged to go for a swim, she repeated her warning, stressing that equation of Bobby and one white car equalling one lifeless Frank. Thank God, Floss breathed, that nothing had happened on this occasion, but to keep tempting fate in this way, well, that was just foolhardy and extremely dangerous.

Bobby must have brooded and worried over her curse, then as she continued to turn it over in her mind, she came up with a simple and drastic solution to forestall its fulfilment. As she saw it, if there were no car there could be no possibility of Floss's premonition coming true – and that was why, in the dead of night when everyone else was asleep, she sneaked out and set fire to this instrument of doom. By the time anyone became aware of what was happening, the jinxed car was fully ablaze. Naturally, Frank was very upset at this wilful destruction, and just as naturally, Floss and Neville guessed who the culprit was. Confronting Bobby, Neville forced the admission from her, then reminding her that arson was a serious criminal offence, suggested that reparations should be made to Frank for the loss of his car which was not only jinxed but uninsured.

Rather than reveal to Frank who was responsible for torching his car by offering the money, comprising Bobby's savings with the additional amount made up from Neville's own, outright, it was decided between them that the donation should be made anonymously – and this, to the mystification of Frank and everyone else, was done through the uncomplicated procedure of placing it in an envelope and leaving it in the Fletchers' letter box, again in the dead of night when everyone else was asleep.

So, completely bamboozled by the windfall that had come in an envelope addressed to him, and receiving no answers to his many questions on this constant theme, Frank bought his new car, also white, and the plans went ahead for the wedding without this additional worry, among so many other worries, to plague him.

At this point, with Frank still trying to find a job while

he was getting the caravan ready for him and Roo to move into after the wedding, that event now came once more into focus. Roo's kicking baby had aroused Bobby's suspicions. Brett had appeared on the scene to be fobbed off by Roo's promise to hand the baby over to him at some time in the future, and Aunt Morag had tried in vain to dissuade Roo from going through with the ceremony which she thinks will be a terrible mistake, Aunt Morag being in a position to know, highly placed as she is in the legal profession which has brought her into contact with, among the sundry preoccupations of her calling, the domestic desolation that can be caused by a marriage ill-conceived, (even when the baby is not).

Also, in the meantime, Roo had selected her wedding dress with the help of Aunt Morag who is well-supplied with credit cards, and had chosen her bridesmaids. The wedding reception had been arranged, the menu had been gone over very thoroughly, more with an eye to economy than anything else. The big day approached, and there was some excitement among the people most directly concerned; with the exception of Bobby Simpson who intended to steer well clear of the ceremony to spare herself so much heartache at seeing the young man she loves marrying a young woman she is quite certain doesn't love him.

The big day approached, then all of a sudden it had arrived and Floss McPhee for one will be glad when it is over because, with that dream still vivid in her mind, she had been left with the impression that Frank and Roo had not been married when the events predicted took place. For her own part, now that the big day has arrived, Roo is suddenly jittery and plagued with doubts.

The bride is nervous and the groom is nervous – and Floss is suddenly petrified when, for the first time, she sees Frank's new white car standing outside the church in the sunlight. Not only the white car of her dream which she thought had been destroyed when Bobby set fire to it, but with those selfsame licence plates that Frank had retrieved from the burnt-out shell of the other vehicle. Her feelings of disaster are only slightly allayed when she learns that Tom Fletcher had insisted upon acting as chauffeur both before and after the ceremony, having decided this when Pippa, in whom Floss had finally confided, had told him of the dream and its alarming significance. He hadn't really believed the dream had such a significance, but had agreed to do the driving – just to be on the safe side, he had said. Floss wasn't sure that that was the answer; in a situation like this, she knew that anything could happen.

And it did happen – just as Floss had predicted it would. The white car, Frank and Bobby came together in that one crucial and explosive sequence of events. It was just as it had appeared in Floss's dream.

Until a few moments before that fateful encounter, it had all gone smoothly enough inside the church. The organ had played, and the congregation had settled in their seats. Frank had waited nervously at the altar with his best man and foster-brother, Steve Mathieson, and he tried not to show the nervousness he felt. In her white, lacy wedding dress, Roo had walked up the aisle on the arm of her father who was to give her away. The service had began, and eventually reached the point where Roo was asked if she would take this man, Frank, as her lawfully wedded husband, to have and to hold, to love and to cherish, and all the rest of it. She opened her mouth, then closed it again. The silence stretched uncomfortably, the waiting congregation shifted restlessly on their hard wooden seats and looked at each other. Querying murmurs could be heard running along the pews, and the clergyman's smile was becoming quite fixed. Roo opened her mouth again, closed it again, then shook her head. There was an audible gasp in the church when it was realized that for some reason or another Roo had changed her mind at the very last moment.

And indeed she had changed her mind. She couldn't go through with it. All the thinking she had done, all the soul-searching and wrestling with her conscience that had been spurred by Aunt Morag's admonishments, was now resolved into a definite plan of action – or, to be more precise, a plan of inaction as she wished to proceed no further on from the point just reached. She kept shaking her head; tears brimmed in her eyes as she whispered those few words to Frank that sent him, angry and confused, totally distraught, running back down the aisle to the front of the church, down the steps and into the white car with its resurrected licence plates, which was waiting outside.

The words Roo had whispered to him in front of the altar, and which had sent him running down the central aisle of the church, quite oblivious to the startled exclamations of the well-wishers who were in attendance; those words which had had an immediate and stunning effect on him and sent him speeding off in that white car of his, were, simply, to the effect that the baby she was carrying, which might have kicked a couple of times during the abruptly terminated ceremony, was not his. Whispered words to be sure, but packing in them all the powered punch of a steam hammer.

So there, for the moment, it stood. In the church, Roo, having dissolved into tears, was being comforted by people who had no idea what this was all about; outside, a bitter and angry Frank was speeding away in his new car without any idea where he was heading. Now all that was needed for the picture to be completed was Bobby Simpson who had stayed away from the ceremony because of the heartache she knew this would bring her, and of course had no idea what had just occurred inside the church.

And it was at this point that Bobby now made her appearance with drastic consequences – Bobby who was walking disconsolately along the street in the belief that it was now done, that Frank and Roo were now man and wife despite all her efforts not to make it so. She was walking sadly along the street towards the beach when she heard the car coming along the street towards her at high speed. She looked, and she recognized the car. She saw Frank behind the wheel, and instinctively stepped out onto the road to hail him . . .

So far all the elements of Floss's dream had fallen into place. The car was exactly as Floss had seen it, twisted crumpled metal against the tree towards which it had swerved to avoid Bobby; Frank's body lying inert in the wreckage; and Bobby screaming and generally showing other signs of panic while the sound of tearing metal and breaking glass was still loud in her ears.

But there was one element of this picture that was not as strong as it had been in Floss's dream, nor as originally depicted in her tarot cards, shortly to be destroyed by Neville McPhee because they had brought nothing but trouble and caused a lot of worry. It is this element that waxed and waned, as Frank's condition waxed and waned on the operating table in the Loxton hospital, waning more than waxing at one stage so that for a while there it was touch and go, with Frank barely clinging onto life. And it was Frank's life, this tenacious clinging onto it, that forms the indistinction. In the cards, then later in her dream, Floss had seen Death; but Death, although hovering nearby, was still being kept at bay through the wonders of medical science, while outside in the waiting room friends and loved ones tried without much success not to fear the worst.

If Roo blamed her Aunt Morag for forcing her into the position of telling Frank the truth, Bobby blamed only herself. She was the one who carried the curse; she was the jinx and the cause of Frank's desperate struggle for life. Her first reaction was to disappear from Summer Bay altogether, and she had actually set out to hitch-hike to the city where she wouldn't be a bother to anyone, when she was picked up by Donald Fisher, the school headmaster, and brought back to the town after her disappearance had been noted and he had driven out to look for her. She offered no resistance; she was much too drained for that.

Roo, too, had had enough of the lies and deception she had perpetrated. She had told Frank the truth just before the accident; now, after the accident, she told her father the whole sorry story, much to Alf's shock, and disappointment in the daughter he had placed on a pedestal. She, too, wanted to leave Summer Bay where she felt she had alienated everyone who knew her beyond the point of forgiveness, and she pleaded with her Aunt Morag to take her back with her to the city where she could make a new start. Morag agreed that this would be the best thing for her confused niece, the reins of whose life she had resolved to take firmly in hand. Yes, she said with the voice of wisdom, in this way she would escape the scandal with which the small town of Summer Bay would soon be buzzing, and which, in the city, would mean nothing at all. The fact that Alf had by now completely disowned his daughter gave added impetus to the move.

For Frank, the worst of the crisis seemed to be over. Bobby maintained a silent vigil by his bed as he lay unconscious; she held his hand and more than once whispered in his ear that she loved him. When she was told by one of the nurses that Frank was lucky to be alive, and that he had, in fact, briefly died on the operating table before being revived, she was hugely relieved because this meant that Floss's prophecy really had been fulfilled. If he *had* died, even if it were only momentarily on the operating table, then that was the end of it, the curse, like Roo, had been removed and the two of them could go forward from there. Yes, she thought as she sat there and held his hand, it had all worked out for the best, most definitely for the best.

Seven

There was a considerable stir in the Fletcher household when Carly Morris burst in on a scene of domestic tranquillity and made her breathless announcement that she had just seen the man who had raped her some months earlier. Everyone stared at her; the statement had been so unexpected. Then Tom Fletcher asked her if she was sure it was the same man. Carly was absolutely positive it was the same man who had picked her up in his car that night when she was hitch-hiking back from Yabbie Creek, driven her to a lonely stretch of bushland then chased her through the undergrowth. It was definitely the same man, she said; she couldn't be mistaken about that; she had just seen him jogging along the beach with Jeff Samuels which, in the eyes of young Steve Mathieson at least, put the seal on his guilt because Jeff Samuels is one of the teachers at the school with a bent towards physical fitness and discipline, and therefore is regarded as something of a fascist by the kids.

Carly was certain that the man she had seen jogging on the beach with Jeff was her attacker, and seeing that he was unable to shake her from that belief, Tom said there was nothing else for it but to inform Bob Barnett, the town policeman. While he and Carly went off to do this, Steve decided to do some investigating of his own and headed off down to the beach where he found the unpopular schoolteacher, clad only in a pair of shorts, kicking a ball around on the sand with another guy, also clad only in a pair of shorts, who bore a slight physical resemblance to him, the explanation for this was soon forthcoming when Jeff Samuels introduced him to Steve as his brother, Gary, who had come up from the city to visit him.

Steve's attitude toward this man who Carly had accused of attacking her was distinctly unfriendly, although he had to admit to himself that the guy didn't exactly look like a rapist, whatever a rapist was supposed to look like. He appeared quite clean-cut and straightforward. But if Carly had been so positive. . . Steve worked himself up into a seething anger, he pointed an accusing finger which might well have been that of an avenging angel, there was a tremor in his voice as he denounced this criminal and told him retribution was at hand – much to the astonishment of the said criminal and his brother who could only gape at him as he stalked off across the sand away from them.

Bob Barnett's approach, on the other hand, was much more cautious. As he told Carly when she reported to him the presence of the malefactor in Summer Bay, there was only her word against his to go on – and, he went on to remind her, the description she had given of her attacker at the time had been quite vague, certainly not strong enough to stand up in a court of law with the lack of any other evidence. All the same, he offered to have a quiet talk with this man and form his own opinion – it was the best he could do.

Bob Barnett's opinion formed during this quiet talk

with Gary Samuels was that he was definitely not the man. This was backed up by Jeff Samuels' claim that as the day of the attack was also his brother's birthday, the two of them had spent that afternoon and evening celebrating the occasion in each other's company. He was quite prepared to testify to that.

No, definitely not the man, Bob reported back to the Fletchers. He had been impressed by his sincerity and the fact that he had a cast-iron alibi. It was obviously a case of mistaken identity, and he had no intention of pursuing the matter.

But Carly was not prepared to accept this, she knew she was right, that there had been no mistake in the identity of her attacker. She was also stung by what she saw as a gross injustice – she had been virtually accused of being a liar while the man who had done that horrendous thing to her was allowed to remain on the loose, to prey on any other young girl who might fall into his clutches – and this was something she was determined to prevent in any way she could. Bob Barnett's refusal to act had made her an extremely bitter and disappointed young lady.

They tried to warn her to drop the matter, not to go around the place making slanderous remarks about a man who was most likely innocent of the crime of which she was accusing him. It would only lead to trouble, they tried to tell her. Tom and Pippa spoke to her about it, Jeff Samuels was more determinedly hostile in his warning when Steve and Carly encountered him as they walked along the beach one afternoon. But Carly just wouldn't let go; she was like a terrier with a bone which she shook and worried and gnawed incessantly.

Gary Samuels was made to feel highly uncomfortable

and embarrassed by this story that was being circulated about him around the town – and it was one to excite a tremendous amount of interest in those places where people gathered, like the pub and the bowling club. Whenever Gary Samuels made an appearance, people nudged each other and made disparaging comments, or looked quickly away after having registered the appearance of a rapist still on the loose. Thanks to Carly, Gary Samuels was the object of the closest scrutiny.

It became so awkward for him that he decided to make a direct approach to Carly's foster-parents, calling at the Fletcher house one morning to find only Pippa at home which suited his purpose as much as if Tom had been there as well – perhaps even more – as he was able to exert his considerable charm on the lady, who in no time at all found herself to be greatly impressed by the reasonableness of his approach to the matter of Carly's accusations, just as much as she was by his clean-cut good looks and his fine manners. When he asked her if she would agree to his meeting Carly to discuss the problem in a rational way, she said she would talk to the girl about it but held out no promise of success.

When she and Tom, whose support she had enlisted in the meantime, did have an opportunity to bring up the subject with Carly that evening over the dinner table, there was quite a scene in the Fletcher household. Carly threw a tantrum; she also threw a plate at the wall where it shattered into about a dozen pieces. She stormed and raged, and accused her foster-parents of nothing less than base treachery by having dealings behind her back with the man who had done such terrible things to her. No, No, No, she screamed about as many times as there were shattered pieces of dinner plate, she would not talk to him, never, ever, definitely in the negative, making her position abundantly clear before rushing out of the house and almost straight into the arms of the subject of her adamant refusals, who was either making his way to the house to see Carly, or was waiting outside in the hope of seeing her. But for whatever reason Gary Samuels was in the immediate neighbourhood, Carly ran slap-bang into him.

He did his best to get through to her, he tried hard to reason with her, to make her see that he couldn't have been the man who had attacked her that night, but Carly was having none of that. Now she was accusing him directly to his face, showing her bitterness and scorn for the man she regarded as a monster, never mind his clean-cut looks and fine manners which were only just persiflage. In the face of this onslaught, it was hardly surprising that Gary Samuels' patience began to wear thin – or as Carly would put it, that the mask began to slip to reveal the true nature of the beast beneath. He became angry with her, his voice hardened, his eyes narrowed. He told her that what she was doing would only backfire on herself and she would be sorry. To Carly, this was a threat that proved the evil make-up of the man, she was quite chilled by it.

As it was by now clear to her that there would be no help forthcoming from the adult quarter, where she was being regarded as some sort of neurotic, Carly enlisted the aid of Steve to get Gary Samuels off her back, which was what he promised to do, already having made up his mind that the man was as guilty as hell. If anyone was to nail the guy, he vowed, he was the one who would do it because no one likes to tangle with someone who is as proficient at karate as Steve is, even more so now than he was then, having kept it up as an activity.

So, emboldened by his prowess in the noble art, Steve sought out Carly's tormentor – or rather, came across him as he was leaving Ailsa Hogan's supermarket, with a plastic shopping bag full of groceries. He told him to stay well clear of Carly at risk of being given a first-hand demonstration of Steve's karate ability. Having delivered this ultimatum, he was surprised to note that Gary Samuels' reaction was quite different from the one he had expected – that he was not cowed or intimidated by the prospect of Steve's hidden forces being unleashed against him; he showed no signs of nervousness, he made no earnest promise to leave Carly alone; his eyes didn't flicker; his tongue didn't moisten lips that had no appearance of having suddenly gone dry. All he did was to laugh at Steve, incensing him by not taking him at all seriously; provoking those forces that lurked inside him – and the more Gary Samuels laughed at him, the more enraged Steve became. He decided to give the man a lesson he would never forget. He dropped into a preparatory stance; his expression became quite ferocious.

What happened then as he darted and feinted and made a sound that came from deep down in his throat and was not dissimilar to someone gargling, Steve was not quite sure. All he could be certain about was that things had gone wrong somewhere along the line, and that he had ended up flat on his back. For a long time afterwards, he went over the procedures in his mind, rehearsed every move he had taken or thought he had taken, every manoeuvre and tactic – but try as hard as he might, the details remained nothing more than a blur that had been terminated by a painful thump and a suspected broken rib – and to add insult to injury, Gary Samuels, still smiling and looking quite unruffled, was offering him his hand to help him regain his feet. Groaning and grimacing, Steve allowed himself to be so helped to his feet, because he didn't think he would make it otherwise. It was then that Gary Samuels laughingly reminded Steve of the first and basic rule of unarmed combat, which is to remember that there is always someone better and faster than you are, in this case meaning Gary Samuels who had just given an effective demonstration of the rule.

Now, more than ever, Steve was convinced that this guy, Gary Samuels, was the rapist. If there had been little doubt of it in his mind before, there was none whatsoever now, particularly as he recalled the malicious glint in Samuels' eyes just before everything happened in a rush and he ended up on the pavement. It was the hard glint of a killer, of a rapist, of a man accustomed to getting his own way who didn't care who he trampled on to get it.

Between them, Steve and Carly gave much thought to how they could trick Gary Samuels into delivering the goods – that is, how they might get him to confess he was the person they both knew him to be and which everyone else needed to be convinced beyond the shadow of a doubt that he was. When Steve produced a small tape recorder and suggested it might in some way be used to record Samuels' confession – if, of course, they could get him to make one – Carly hedged a little at first but allowed herself to be persuaded that it mightn't be such a bad idea at that – in fact, the more she thought about it the more attractive an idea it became. She agreed to allow herself to be wired up with the recorder before she proceeded to the fateful interview, a rough outline of which, if not the precise details, had to be worked out.

In the meantime, Gary Samuels was gradually working himself into the good books of a fair majority of people in the town who by now had become more or less convinced that such a clean-cut and well-mannered young man could hardly be a rapist. In fact, in certain quarters he was becoming quite popular.

Armed with the tape recorder, now wired up to Carly inside her clothes where it wouldn't be noticed, she and Steve set out to intercept Gary Samuels just as he was about to go on his regular afternoon jog along the beach. He wasn't pleased to see them; he was even less pleased when they began to ask him provocative questions about the rape and his part in it. It *was* you, wasn't it? You *did* do it, didn't you? I *know* it was you, so there's no point in denying it. So on and so forth, in that vein while the tape recorder whirred silently beneath Carly's blouse.

But Samuels wasn't admitting anything to these two kids who were badgering and harrassing him and trying to make him confess to a serious crime. Instead, he became increasingly more annoyed with them; a deepening frown creased his smooth bronzed brow; the dangerous glint Steve had seen once before appeared in his eye. Finally, as they continued to harry him with questions that were not too far-ranging from the subject to hand, the last of his control snapped and he shouted at them to lay off or by God, he would make them rue the day – or words to that effect. Having threatened assault and mayhem, he then set off on his jog along the beach with probably not as much zest as he had originally had.

He had warned them to lay off and of the dire consequences that would ensue if they did not – and both Carly and Steve were triumphant. To them this was evidence irrefutable, the confession made and recorded. All they needed to do now was bear off their prize to Bob Barnett at the police station, lay it down on the desk before him and say, there you are, there's the evidence, organize the warrant and make the arrest.

But there was no warrant to be issued, or arrest to be effected. When he heard the tape which was a bit scratchy and not altogether clear in parts, particularly when Gary Samuels was shouting at them, and after the rhythmic *bomp-bomp-bomping* sound that underlay and sometimes overlay it all had been identified as Carly's heart-beat, Bob Barnett delivered his own warning to the two amateur bloodhounds. They had done a very wrong thing, he admonished, by recording someone's conversation without their knowledge or consent. Not only was it wrong, he said, but it was against the law. And what did the recording prove, anyway? Only that Gary Samuels was fed up to the back teeth with these constant hammering questions of theirs. Anyone else would have reacted in the same way. He, Bob Barnett, would have lost his temper with them much sooner than Gary Samuels had. As it was, Samuels had every right to press charges against them under State law for this blatant invasion of his privacy.

Both Steve and Carly were feeling quite deflated by the time he had delivered this stern lecture – and once again, Carly discerned conspiracy and betrayal from the older generation, particularly from Tom and Pippa Fletcher who insisted on telling her that on all the evidence that had so far been provided, they had no alternative but to believe that Gary Samuels couldn't have been her attacker. Carly was quite disgusted with this negative approach. She *knew* Gary Samuels was the perpetrator, she couldn't have been more certain in her own mind, and, after all, she had been there at the time. None of the others who were now making all these judgments had been there, none of them had been involved as she had been involved. Pippa did offer one small sop to Carly's feelings, however; she did say that if she was proved wrong, she would never forgive herself.

Some time during that evening there occurred what is generally termed as a Development, the reason Bob Barnett left his house-cum-police station early the following morning with a very grim expression and headed for the beach where Gary Samuels was preparing to set out on his early morning run. It was this Development that caused him to interrupt Gary Samuels' running plans. It was a Development, he said, of the most serious order, and concerned the attack on a young girl that had taken place during the night in the vicinity of Yabbie Creek. This attack had been a particularly vicious one, and in many respects was similar to the one that had been made on Carly. The girl was still recovering in the Loxton hospital, Bob Barnett informed Gary Samuels who was looking increasingly uncomfortable and was sweating a little, even though the sun had some way to go before it reached its full strength, but she had been able to provide a detailed description of her attacker which had formed the basis of the identikit picture Bob Barnett now solemnly produced.

Gary Samuels stared at the picture Bob was holding out at him, and sweated a little more. Yes, he had to concede, there was a likeness, a certain resemblance, but that didn't mean he was the guilty party; the picture was of someone else who just happened to look like him. Bob conceded that there was definitely that possibility, but even so, a positive identification needed to be made, a line-up formed in which Gary Samuels would be a component part so that the victim could pick him out, or not pick him out as her attacker, as the case may be.

When the news of this latest Development spread around the town, and people learned that Gary Samuels was being questioned about it, the general reaction was one of shock. Everyone who had come to form the opinion that Samuels was a nice fellow was now having second thoughts about it. They were bewildered and angry that he should have pulled the wool over their eyes so effectively as he had. They felt swindled and used. Carly Morris, on the other hand, felt totally vindicated. She had been right after all, but until now no one had chosen to believe her. She felt a great sense of relief that it was all over at last. But it wasn't yet over – not quite; there was to be another Development which was to make Carly feel truly awful again.

The message came through while Bob Barnett was questioning Gary Samuels about his movements the previous night, which, unfortunately for Samuels were not as precise as they should have been if his innocence was to be instantly proclaimed. When he answered the telephone, Bob nodded a few times, grunted, made doodles with his pen on the pad in front of him, stared thoughtfully up at the ceiling, stared thoughtfully at Gary Samuels, at the door, at the floor and at the grey metal filing cabinet in the corner. He scratched his head, frowned, nodded and grunted some more, muttered something, then as he replaced the receiver, said to Samuels, 'There's been a Development.'

To be more precise, this 'Development' was another attack on a girl near Yabbie Creek, this time in broad daylight, which had proved to be the perpetrator's downfall, as he had been spotted running away from the scene of the crime; had been chased and tackled; had been apprehended and carted off to the Yabbie Creek police station for questioning.

It was quite a to-do. The town was buzzing with the story for weeks afterwards. Poor Carly – she actually deserved more sympathy than she received as it was quite clear, when she made her positive identification of the rapist, that there was a strong resemblance to Gary Samuels after all, although it couldn't be said that the guilty man looked anywhere near as clean-cut, or possessed such fine manners as the school-teacher's brother, who had resumed his regular jogs along the beach, morning and afternoon, to keep himself fit, and to whom poor Carly, mortified by the recollection of her accusations against him, steeled herself to apologize.

Eight

When Anzac Day comes round every April, virtually the whole town turns out to commemorate the fallen of both World Wars, the Vietnam War and other scraps in between in which our troops have been engaged. Like every other town, small and large, throughout the length and breadth of the country, we have our own Anzac Day procession in Summer Bay, with the local brass and pipe bands providing the beat for the old, and not so old, soldiers, sailors and airmen as they march with their heads held high and their chests bedecked with service medals. Wreaths are laid at the war memorial where the dawn service is always well-attended, and after the march which starts at the lagoon then comes over the hill to run the length of the esplanade before doubling back behind the shops and into the park where another service is held at the war memorial, there are the reunions, generally either at the pub or the bowling club, where reminiscences are exchanged over a glass of beer and sandwiches which have been prepared by members of the Ladies' Guild. It's a fine day, a grand day; it's also a sad day as these former combatants recall their lost comrades.

For the kids of the Fletcher household, it was a day which they didn't look forward to, if only for the reason that this was when their Uncle Danny, Pippa

Fletcher's brother who had been injured rather badly in the Vietnam War, made his annual visit to Summer Bay, which was, too, in the nature of a reunion between him and Tom, who had also served in that campaign.

The kids didn't look forward to their foster-uncle's visit because his experiences in Vietnam had left him a completely shattered man, not only physically but mentally. He was a sour, embittered man, and there was always tension in the house when he was staying with them. That was how it always had been, and this year it wasn't expected to be any different.

Yet, surprisingly enough, it was different. This time, when he arrived in Summer Bay, he was actually quite cheerful for a change. There wasn't the customary gloom, the strong emanation of inner despair which would cow even the most high-spirited among them. There he was, quite bluff and hearty, no gloom, no despondency, just good humour and a smile for everyone because, as he explained to Tom, he had just made a crucial decision about the direction his life was to take from that point on, which was a massive load off his mind.

No despair? No bitterness? He certainly wasn't showing these to anyone this year – but who knew then what was still lodged inside him, what dark burdens were being harboured? Who knew what this crucial decision was that he had just made and claimed to be such a load off his mind? He wasn't telling them – not just yet, anyway.

Anzac Day arrived. There was the dawn service at the war memorial, then the march through the town. It was a bright, warm day; it couldn't have been more perfect for the occasion. In the afternoon, some of Tom's friends gathered at the house for a few drinks, a few jokes and stories, as usual on this holiday.

Normally, this was an occasion for the men only, Tom and these friends of his with their campaign medals and faces that became more flushed with the amount of beer steadily supplied by Tom, were more relaxed in each others' company on this day than they would have been in the presence of women and children who would have put a brake on their comradely exuberance. Pippa Fletcher realized this, and accepted it. Carly also tolerated this exclusion for this one day of the year at least. Bobby Simpson, on the other hand, couldn't come to terms with it, and this year was no different from any other year when her querulous demands to know why she couldn't join the men, drink beer and listen to jokes of questionable taste could be heard from the kitchen where the ladies of the house had retired for the duration and which all but Bobby were probably quite pleased to do.

One female who had no compunction about joining the men, not being aware of any unwritten law and determined only to be a source of comfort and inspiration to Danny, was Celia Stewart who, true to manner and quite unthinkingly, barged straight in through the open back door of the Fletcher house, graciously accepted Pippa's offer of a cup of tea, then proceeded into the room where the menfolk were having a good time. As she entered the room, the conversation faltered a little, straggled somewhat as she made herself comfortable in an armchair, then tapered off into an awkward silence as she beamed happily around at them and said how nice it was to be among men who were enjoying themselves so thoroughly on Anzac Day.

The silence became more strained as she chirped and twittered away about this and that, about matters that were of no real interest to the company assembled, and which caused some of the restless shuffling that then took place, and the odd surreptitious glance at a wristwatch which prompted a muttered exclamation to the effect that, oh, how quickly the time has passed, the wearer didn't realize how late it was, and well, must be getting along, the little woman's waiting, I promised to take her to the bowling club, so on and so forth. A few people just then realized how late it was, time having passed so quickly, always the way when you're enjoying yourself, and decided they had better be moving along. Celia was quite oblivious to the movement around her; she was in deep discussion with Danny, the man to whom she had come to offer her moral support.

In actual fact, she wasn't so much deep in discussion with Danny as listening to him with a dawning expression of horror as he quite matter-of-factly told her a gruesome story, the main purpose of which was to speed up her own departure from the room.

He spared no detail in his description of how a fellow soldier had been blown up by a land mine in Vietnam. He held back no horrific fact, although it is possible he might have been a little over-liberal with his disposition of blood and bone, hair and teeth, fingers and toes. But that didn't matter; his story had the desired effect and Celia fled the room in a state of extreme distress.

What Danny didn't know when he had launched into his narrative was that Celia's fiancé had also been killed by a land mine in Vietnam. His story, embellished or not, had brought it all back to her, and the graphic details of what happened to a person when he was blown up by a land mine had caused her to choke back a scream, had caused the tears to start up in her eyes and send her running out into the kitchen where, slumping onto a chair at the table, she buried her face in her hands and sobbed and sobbed and sobbed, and told Pippa how terrible it was, how awful, and how much she did regret now not having slept with her fiancé, perhaps to bear his child, before he flew off to the war from which he was not to return.

Danny had already had quite an amount to drink when he told Celia his gruesome story. He continued to drink for the rest of the afternoon and well into the night. He sat slumped in his wheelchair, and brooded as he drank, the former good humour he had shown on his arrival now completely gone. He was still there after the others had gone to bed and Pippa came into the living room to say goodnight to him and have a request put to her that was to unsettle her and cause her to spend a sleepless night.

It was Pippa he had really come to see this time, he said, Pippa who had been a nurse and knew what could be done. Already alarmed by his tone which had a hollow, mechanical quality to it, and by the intense way he was staring up at her from his wheelchair, Pippa asked him what he meant. His expression was bleak, his face was pale and drawn as he told her what he meant. She would know of a way to put him out of his misery, he said.

That night, as she lay awake, Pippa pondered on her brother's words and the strangeness of his manner. Of course, he was drunk, she tried to reassure herself;

they were simply the disjointed sentiments of a man who'd had too much to drink and allowed himself to be overcome by despondency, and who would be all right again in the morning when he was sober, bright and cheerful again as he had been all that day – or for *most* of the day before too much alcohol had cast him into a deep and self-pitying gloom. But the more she tried to convince herself of this, the more she was unable to do so. There had been something about him that went deeper than just the liquor he had consumed.

This impression was confirmed when she saw him the following morning after the others had gone about their daily business, the kids to school and Tom to the road-gang on which he had been reinstated. Danny was quite sober now, although the previous day's drinking session had left its legacy in his red-rimmed and bleary eyes, and hands that trembled a little as, with both of them clasped around a mug of strong black coffee, he raised it slowly to his lips. He hadn't shaved, he looked awful. He, too, had spent a restless night, his fitful snatches of sleep throbbing and exploding with the sounds of incessant warfare.

No, he assured Pippa now, he had been quite serious; he was absolutely certain of what he wanted to do; he'd had nothing else to do but sit in his wheelchair day after day and think about it. He'd had enough. He was of no use to anyone. His parents, their parents, his and Pippa's, worked day and night to look after him; they were quite worn out, it was hardly fair that they should devote their lives to him when they should be relaxing and enjoying their retirement, which people said were the best years.

As she listened to him, Pippa became more and more

angry. She was angered by what she could only see as his selfishness in wanting to involve her in the first place, with all the ramifications that was likely to bring in its wake. She was angry with him because of what she perceived to be his total lack of courage in wishing to give up the struggle, then having decided that, not having the strength of character to carry it through alone. She was very, very angry with him, and refused to listen to him when he tried to explain the depths of his feelings, his bitterness, the sense of uselessness and all the rest of it.

If anyone could talk him out of this self-destructive mood, it would be Tom. Danny thought the world of Tom. He would at least listen to anything Tom had to say. But Tom was at work and wouldn't be home until later that afternoon. At the same time, the more she thought about it, she couldn't be sure that Danny wasn't just seeking attention for himself. Her instinct began to tell her that that might well be the case – or perhaps this was just wishful thinking on her part. Tom would know.

Ailsa Hogan agreed with her when they discussed it, because Pippa desperately needed to talk to someone about it before Tom arrived home, and Ailsa was her best friend. Ailsa thought that even if Danny was only grandstanding, he was still probably in need of professional help to snap him out of his dark mood. Again, the only person who could persuade him to see this would be Tom. Pippa agreed that the best course of action would be for the three of them – that is, Danny, Tom and herself – to sit down together and discuss the matter calmly and rationally.

The conversation with Ailsa had taken place at the supermarket. She had left Danny alone in the house after extracting from him a promise that he wouldn't do anything rash during her absence. In any case, she had told him, the kids would soon be home from school to keep him company. But when she arrived home, leaving Ailsa, she discovered he wasn't there, although it wasn't until she learned from one of the other kids that he had gone up to Stewart's Point with Carly and Lynn in search of insects of some form or other for Lynn's school biology project that she became anxious and hurried off in that direction after them in the desperate hope that she wouldn't be too late, and that her brother hadn't already hit on the simple expedient of rolling his wheelchair and himself over the high cliff in which the point abruptly terminated, onto the rocks below.

To her huge relief, she found him still intact when she arrived there quite out of breath – and seeing that he hadn't rolled the wheelchair and himself over the cliff, became angry with him again. Sending the girls home with their assorted insects in a box, she rounded furiously on her unhappy brother who, when she arrived, had been sitting close to the edge of the cliff in his wheelchair and gazing out to sea. How dare he? she demanded. What right had he? she asked. If he wanted to kill himself, that was all right with her – but to do it in front of the kids, to allow them to witness the fatal fall, then that was something else again. She was livid, quite ropeable; she said things she didn't really mean, she was so angry – even when she gestured towards the edge of the cliff and in her rage dared him to go ahead and do it if that was what was on his mind because she didn't care anymore what he did with his own life. She still didn't really mean it, but it wasn't until she was home again and had calmed down a little over a restoring cup of tea that she realized the enormity of what she had dared him to do.

She had left him there, near the edge of the cliff; he had begged her to leave him alone. He was ashamed, he said. He hadn't had the courage to go through with it, he said. He didn't have the courage now. He would be all right, he assured her, she didn't have to worry about him; he would follow her shortly in his wheelchair; all he wanted now was to be left alone for a while; he wanted to think.

But he wasn't back by the time Tom arrived home in his dusty overalls and asked where Danny was. Pippa had already begun to become anxious again when Danny didn't come home as soon as he had been expected, although she didn't know how much time he required to sit up there on the point alone and think matters through. But now she was becoming very worried again. Tom, too, was worried, but not because of Danny's suicidal frame of mind, which Pippa now refrained from mentioning, as she refrained from mentioning her angry confrontation with him, he was just worried that something might have happened to him while he was out.

Having told Tom that she had last seen Danny up on the point where he had originally gone with Lynn and Carly on their insect-hunting expedition, and that he had expressed the desire to be by himself for a while, the point was obviously the first place to look. But as they approached it, with Pippa already fearing the worst – that Danny had manged to find the courage to go through with it after all – there was no sign of him or his wheelchair. They moved on up the grassy slope towards the edge of the cliff, Pippa now finding it difficult to breathe in her apprehension of what they might discover. They moved up to the edge of the cliff; they stood right on the edge of the cliff and peered down. Pippa gasped and closed her eyes; Tom muttered an exclamation.

There is still no fencing at the top of this cliff which makes it quite a dangerous place to be if one is not careful. One could easily lean out too far to see what lies below and lose their footing. Skylarking kids could also venture too close to the edge, then find it's too late to regain their balance. Anything can happen if one steps too close to the edge – a rock or a lump of earth falling away beneath them being another instance of what could occur if one is not cautious – but so far, because people are generally careful about approaching too close to the edge, no serious misadventure has taken place on our cliff although it falls sheerly away to the rocks below and the waves that wash over the rocks and between them, and are now washing over the mangled and twisted remains of Danny's wheelchair.

But where was Danny? There was no sign of Danny. Had he been washed out to sea? It was unlikely because the water where the wreckage of the wheelchair could be discerned was much too shallow? Had he been thrown clear as the wheelchair plummeted to be lying further along the base of the cliff, just as crumpled and as twisted? They looked, but they saw nothing. Pippa, clutching Tom's arm, felt quite faint. So where *was* Danny?

It was a question that was still being asked a couple of hours later by the rescue services that had been mobilized from Summer Bay and Yabbie Creek to search for the presumed body which remained undiscovered by any boat or by the helicopter that hovered along the coast in the immediate vicinity, and eluded even the strongest binoculars that were ranged up and down the same area. The same question was also being asked in the town, in the pub and in the bowling club, and as usual, theories were offered as to what might have happened to Danny's body. Someone suggested that he had been caught up in a thick tangle of seaweed. The possibility that he had been taken by a shark gained some popularity as it generally does when broached. But whatever theory was produced, Danny's body was most certainly not.

By now, Pippa was completely distraught. She blamed only herself for what had happened – she might just as well have pushed the wheelchair over the cliff herself – but still she didn't tell Tom what had passed between her and Danny. She didn't dare admit her guilt to him.

Then, while all this activity was going on; while questions were being asked and theories offered in abundance, lo and behold who should turn up out of the blue and with a sheepish smile, but the object of the excitement himself. Pippa gaped at him; Tom gaped at him; the kids all gaped at him as Alf and Celia Stewart helped him into the house and into an armchair. Pippa herself slumped onto a chair. It was all proving too much for her.

Of course, Danny had his own story now that he was back from the dead, and this was the one he had told Alf and Celia, who had found him and taken him back to their house; he said that the wheelchair, its brake not on at the time, had rolled over the cliff just as he climbed out of it to sun himself on the grass – which may or may not have been the simple truth of the matter, but the fact that he had allowed himself to remain for so long at the Stewart house without informing anyone where he was, even though he must have known that people, Pippa in particular, would be out of their minds with worry, was to arouse the suspicion that there was some malicious intent. It wasn't too difficult to imagine that Danny, wanting to get back at Pippa for the way she had lashed out at him, had contrived to push the wheelchair over the cliff, then remained at the Stewart house long enough for Pippa to go through agonies over her earlier hard-heartedness. This was something that passed through Pippa's mind, anyway, and yet again, and much to the mystification of the others who witnessed the scene that followed, she lost her temper with Danny who thought he could treat her this way and get away with it.

She yelled at him and called him names, she accused him again of being selfish and manipulative, and shook her finger in front of his nose. She was trembling with anger, which was largely a reaction to the strained and upsetting couple of hours when she had honestly believed him to be dead as a result of her own thoughtlessness. As she continued to rail, Tom finally stepped in and tersely told her to stop carrying on like this, he couldn't understand why she was acting in this way, it was totally uncalled for.

Even then, Pippa could have told him the reason for her outburst, but she didn't. She knew that if she did tell him the truth of what had passed between her and her brother, the close bond between him and Tom would be broken – and she didn't want that at all. She had to remain silent, for the sake of their friendship which was very important to them both.

She also had to live with the knowledge that one day Danny would at last find the courage to do what he had threatened. Perhaps it would be sooner; perhaps it would be later; she couldn't know when. But one day . . .

Nine

The one great shadow that hangs over most of us here in Summer Bay is the ever-present prospect of the developers moving in, so that before we know what's happening the place will be full of hotels, motels and high-rise apartment blocks to cast a shadow over the beach as well as over our lives. Then there would be shopping malls and fancy boutiques, bars and nightclubs with garish neon lighting and poker machines, maybe even a gambling casino which would be the kiss of death to our quiet, even sleepy, existence here on the coast because there are people who believe that this would be the thin edge of the wedge which, widening, would bring in all sorts of other undesirable elements. Before long, the place would be teeming with strange characters at whom you wouldn't want to look even sideways. The town would become noisy and shrill, and just keep spreading outwards until it was joined up with all the other towns in the district and eventually become a sprawling extension of the city itself. Things would start happening that had never happened before in Summer Bay, and the beach would be useless, anyway, because of the shadows cast by those high-rise apartment blocks that have been put up in such a hurry to capitalize on the boom everyone keeps talking about, and will probably end up in the ocean, in any event, in due course of time when after a long spell of bad weather it is suddenly found that there is no longer any beach left. In short, our town stands in every danger of becoming, God help us, a . . . *resort*.

It has happened to other places; you see examples of it everywhere along the coast. What has once been a small village tucked away in some bay or inlet is now a brash and untidy conglomerate of those hotels, motels, high-rise apartment blocks, bars, nightclubs and takeaway food outlets that cast their shadows over our peaceful community. People call this progress; we call it a nightmare.

No, we would like things to carry on the way they are, never mind the progress which is just another name for chaos to our way of thinking; we don't want to be spoilt, we're quite happy without pizza parlours and pinball machines, we have no pining desire for boat marinas, high priced French restaurants and revolving ones on top of look-out towers, we can do quite happily without multi-story car parks, traffic lights and swarms of half-naked people clogging the footpaths. We just want to remain as we are, easy-going and tolerant, even as we were when Roo Stewart turned up one day with a Chinese boyfriend, which threw Alf Stewart into a fit, and thankfully wouldn't have worked out, anyway, with this boy's parents also having a fit because they already had a nice Chinese girl picked out for him to marry according to the time-honoured custom.

Now, having said all that, it does happen more often than not that inducements can be made that are quite irresistible, and bring them the realization that one is actually sitting on a gold-mine. The temptation becomes too strong to withstand, and the assurances offered by smooth-talking salesmen that while the character of the town would be basically unchanged, the place would be up-graded a little with, of course, an eye to the environment which, naturally, would be the uppermost consideration, are more readily accepted by those who have already half made up their mind to accept the offer and move on to some other part of the coast that has not as yet been singled out as a holiday paradise.

Now it seemed that Summer Bay had been singled out to become the next holiday paradise, and from the highly coloured, highly illustrated brochure that was making the rounds it wouldn't have looked too bad as a holiday paradise, even if hardly recognizable as Summer Bay. This glossy brochure had been printed by a group calling itself Macklin Enterprises which had already set up an office in the town.

The head of this organization was one Gordon Macklin who had already made a mint of money in other developments such as apartment buildings, shopping centres and car parks. Now he had his eye on Summer Bay, which had the residents fairly well divided as to the rights and wrongs of it, some saying that it would be good for the town, meaning that the property values would rocket skyward, while others, like Ailsa Hogan, had their very definite doubts as to whether they needed a holiday paradise and all that would bring into their midst. The discussions on the matter at times became quite heated. Those who foresaw an upward leap in the price of the property called themselves progressive, while most of the others called themselves nothing at all; they just wanted to be left alone.

As was to be established, Gordon Macklin, the

property tycoon, had an additional reason for making Summer Bay the base for his next operation – and in a roundabout sort of way this was a family reason because now it can be revealed that his son, Brett, is the same Brett who is the father of Roo Stewart's still expected baby. Brett, who had come to Summer Bay to be close to Roo, also back from the city, had virtually talked his father into transforming Summer Bay into a summer paradise, had been put in charge of the plans for the development while the older man tended to his wide-ranging business interests elsewhere.

Because Roo had come to love Frank, and because Frank was still in love with Roo with whom he has become reconciled despite the way she had almost tricked him into marrying her, it was quite understandable that there should be friction between Frank and Brett Macklin, the father of Roo's baby. The antagonism was definitely there, and, if anything, became more intense after Brett made him an offer he could hardly refuse, which was apparently designed to allow him to gain the upper hand in a relationship that was now one of employer and employee, since Frank had been so desperate to find work and that despite his misgivings about Brett's motives in offering him a job in the first place, he was unable to resist the attractive terms that would result in his name being added to the payroll of Macklin Enterprises. Also, and probably not less importantly, it placed him in a position where he could sabotage the development plans from within, or at least find out, from the inside of the operation, just what the little schemer, Brett Macklin, was planning. It was also partly for this purpose, at the instigation of Ailsa Hogan, who was dead set against any development taking place in Summer Bay, that he had accepted the job.

At that stage, the proposed plans for Summer Bay had not yet been made public. The nicely illustrated brochure that had been printed to accompany the prospectus prepared by the company to attract investment in the Summer Bay project had not as yet made the rounds – nor was it intended that it should make the rounds until that investment had been guaranteed. So it would have remained if Frank, now ensconced in the company's Summer Bay office and therefore privy to papers and documents and other things that were going on, hadn't come across this brochure on Brett's desk where it had been carelessly left while he was away from the office, and shown it to Ailsa who was quite stunned by the enormity of the changes that were being planned, and to ensure that everyone else would be as stunned as she was, had made sure it fell into the hands of the local newspaper over in Loxton.

For the local newspaper, it was grist for the mill. It was a front page story which was carried over onto the two succeeding pages and warranted an editorial comment that was hardly encouraging. Brett was furious when he saw the story with its accompanying illustrations, which had been lifted straight from the brochure. He yelled and swore, and demanded to know the name of the culprit who had supplied the damning details to the press. He didn't think to suspect Frank who, of course, denied all knowledge of the leakage, instead his suspicions homed in on Ailsa who had been so vocal in her opposition, and who now was the subject of a telephone call he made to his father, the gist of which was that a way needed to be found to draw this meddling woman's attention from their scheme. How this was to be achieved was another question. Ailsa's blood was up, she was on the war-path; she was fast becoming a one-woman crusader. She even went so far as to have a circular printed with her name on it, calling for the residents to man the barricades against the proposed development.

In the Fletcher household opinions about the development were divided, as they were in the pub and bowling club, and just about everywhere else in the town. Tom Fletcher was in favour of the project because he was convinced it would attract business to the caravan park, Pippa, on the other hand, who didn't believe that the Macklins had the interests of the community at heart, and therefore didn't trust them, accused him of shortsightedness. Others adopted a wait and see attitude; Neville McPhee, for instance, said he wanted to hear what the developers had to say about their plans before he made up his mind.

When Frank himself seemed to be coming round to the idea that the Macklin proposal might well have its benefits for the community, Ailsa was disappointed in him, and refused to listen to him any further on this contentious subject. She was also disappointed in Alf, who had been furious with her over the circular she had distributed. By printing such a document under her own name, and in obvious opposition to his own view which she had made widely known, she had made him a laughing stock in the town, he said.

This serious difference of opinion between Alf and Ailsa was something that could be exploited by the Macklins to isolate her even further – and it was, with the help of Alf's daughter, Roo, whose resentment towards Ailsa, who presumed to take the place of Roo's late mother, had in no way diminished. Since she had returned to Summer Bay, she had made up the quarrel with her father who, more than simply re-owning her, had restored her to that pedestal from which she had been swept, with the revelation that Frank was not the father of her baby. Apart from her feelings towards Ailsa, it appeared that Brett exercised a subtle control over her through his employment of Frank which, he must have implied, could be terminated at any moment if things didn't go Brett's way. Anyway, when Alf was persuaded to invest some money in the Macklin venture, the rift between him and Ailsa was widened even further.

The next move was up to Ailsa. She made it by calling in a conservationist from the city to assess the environmental impact the development would have on Summer Bay if it went through, which she was determined it wouldn't. She had high hopes for this conservationist who had a beard and went about the task of assessment with admirable thoroughness. He circled the lagoon and looked thoughtful, he examined the reeds that fringed the lagoon and nodded to himself, he studied the pelicans and other forms of bird life, and seemed quite satisfied, he climbed sand dunes and clambered over rocks, he went for a swim in the surf and ran along the beach afterwards, he had lunch, then strolled out to the point, he looked for rare forms of wildlife, and found none; he drove out to the National Park and drove back again by the inland route; he scribbled furiously in his notebook; in short, he seemed to know what he was doing, and Ailsa was greatly impressed.

Alf was out when Ailsa bore her bearded conservationist in triumph back to his house so that he could hear the report at first-hand. Roo, however, was there, and was introduced by Ailsa to her new friend who, because of other commitments not necessarily of an environmental nature, soon left them and his report to be studied at leisure by Alf when he returned. When he had gone, Roo predicted direly that her father would go through the roof when he learned that Ailsa had taken it into her head to bring such a man into the picture and so complicate the issue even more. For her part, Ailsa was quite confident that Alf would listen to reason once he'd had time to peruse the material that had been left for him.

Brett Macklin had already been told by Roo of this development when Ailsa went to his office to tell him that the conservationist had recommended modifications to his development proposal, and refused to listen to her; in fact, he became quite terse with her. Alf, on the other hand, did at least read the report before pronouncing it to be his opinion that the character of Summer Bay would not be jeopardized by the venture into which he had invested a considerable sum of money. Again, Ailsa showed her disappointment. The rift between them was just as wide as ever.

Not daunted by this opposition, Ailsa's next idea was to call a public protest meeting, and she booked the church hall for this purpose before going to the trouble of having posters printed to advertize the event. An unexpected ally she found at this time was Donald Fisher, the school headmaster, who, agreeing with Ailsa that although such developments might work out all right in other locations, they would be the kiss of death as far as Summer Bay was concerned, offered to help her stick up the posters at various strategic points around the town

– and it was while they were sticking up these posters that they found, to their horror, that a double-cross had been neatly effected by Alf Stewart who had just had his own posters printed to advertize his own public meeting which he had arranged to support the development proposals, and what was more, proclaimed these posters that had already been stuck up at strategic points around the town, the venue for this meeting was the selfsame church hall where Ailsa's own protest meeting had been booked, and moreover, had been booked for the selfsame time. It was a stab in the back, a neat betrayal which made Ailsa livid, not only with Alf but with the people responsible for allowing the hall to be double-booked in this way, denoting a carefree attitude to say the least.

What she saw as another betrayal was in store for her when the conservationist fellow on whom she had relied to provide incontrovertible evidence at her meeting that the development would be detrimental to the environment of Summer Bay backed out with the excuse that he was unable to help in the campaign owing to pressure of work, which immediately made Ailsa suspicious. She suspected foul play, that the conservationist had been nobbled, had been made an offer he had been unable to refuse. She made a bee-line straight for Brett Macklin's office to confront him with her suspicions.

But instead of confirming those suspicions, Brett Macklin simply laughed at her and told her that she was obviously succumbing to some sort of paranoia that made her think all the time of conspiracies. He then dropped a gentle but unmistakable threat to Ailsa's economic security by mentioning quite casually that he and his father were debating whether a supermarket should be included in the development plans – the obvious implication here being that Ailsa's own business would be left out in the cold if she didn't cease her opposition to the project.

As it turned out, Alf was just as furious by the double-booking of the church hall as Ailsa was. It hadn't been done deliberately, he assured her; the man who had taken the booking had assumed that he was merely confirming the booking that had already been made by Ailsa rather than arranging a meeting of his own. But what was done, he added with a shrug, was done; he certainly had no intention of postponing his own meeting now that the posters had been printed and stuck up around the town; Ailsa would have to change her own arrangements, that was all. He suggested she might have it in her house which would easily accommodate the few people who would turn up for it, a touch of humour Ailsa was quite unable to appreciate.

Brett's implied threat to Ailsa's business was another matter, however; Alf didn't think that was funny at all when she told him of it, and finding Brett in his office, angrily warned him not to do anything that would put that business in jeopardy, firmly over-riding Brett's protest that he was merely telling Ailsa that he was *thinking* of opening a supermarket, that was all, it was a free country, anybody could open a supermarket if they wished, there was certainly no question of intimidation on his part. All the same, Brett was left a little rattled by the encounter, and decided to offer Roo a chance to stir up things even further.

As usual, Roo played her part with the utmost conviction, the reason why she got away with what she did as often as she did, and she had no trouble convincing her father that she had overheard Brett on the telephone to *his* father, and from certain remarks he had made, had divined that Alf was to be no longer part of the project. Once again, Alf headed off to the Macklin office in search of clarification, only to be told by Brett that Macklin senior was becoming thoroughly fed up with all the vacillation and interference that was being set in the way of the project and didn't think that Alf's continued involvement was worth all the trouble. In other words, he wanted Alf out of it. Naturally, Alf was most upset by this, and blamed an unrepentant Ailsa for wrecking his chances of making a fortune.

Much to Roo's delight, the ensuing row was very intense, very bitter – and provided a classic instance of things being said that shouldn't have been said, but having been said were too late to retract or otherwise repair the damage. What Alf said during this row and which was to put their relationship on an extremely rocky footing for a while just slipped out without thinking, all he wanted to do was lash out at her in his rage, to hurt her as he himself felt he had been hurt. But he had no sooner uttered those fateful words than he realized that with them he had gone too far – but by then, of course, it was too late, the damage had been done.

Those fateful words that Ailsa couldn't bring herself to forgive for a long time to come; those fateful words so blindly delivered by Alf in his rage were prompted by Ailsa's remark that he was behaving just like her father if only in his chauvinistic attitude towards women. It was like a red rag to the bull that Alf had become. It was provocation in the extreme; it was the limit. 'Then I'd better not turn my back on you, had I?' Alf retorted, then immediately realized what a terrible thing he had said, and that this reference to Ailsa's desperate action so many years before to save her terrified mother from the brutalities of her drunken father by plunging the kitchen carving knife into his back, could only open up old wounds that had never been properly healed. Alf was stricken with remorse by what he had just said; Ailsa was unforgiving. Roo – dear, sweet Roo – was triumphant.

Ten

Ambition can be a fine and noble quality to have. Carried forward by ambition, great things can be achieved. Sometimes ambition can be turned in the wrong direction with the result that not such fine things are accomplished even if it does enrich the possessor of it. The sights can be set high, or directed to a more immediate goal – but in just about every case, the object of ambition is success, fame and riches.

People are driven by different ambitions. It is Tom and Pippa's ambition, for instance, to get out of the financial rut they are in, although it can't be said that things are looking too bad at the present. But they could be better, and now that there's a baby on the way the worries won't be over for some time to come.

The Macklins, father and son, have the ambition to make Summer Bay a holiday paradise, and it is Ailsa's immediate aim not to have Summer Bay turned into a holiday paradise, but to have it remain as it is – and in any event, now that the relationship between her and Alf has reached breaking point, she no longer feels that there is much of a future for her here in the town. Alf, of course, wishes he had left certain things unsaid, but that is hardly an ambition. For the moment, however, he sees his future tied up with the development and is resolved to make himself once more part of it.

Roo's baby is still on the way, kicking more solidly now, and it is to be supposed that she does entertain hopes for its future. But that is in no way certain; Brett is still hovering around her with his aim of assuming custody of the child when it is born. What could be said more positively about Roo, however, is that she is now quite convinced she is in love with Frank – and here, her ambition takes on a little more substance. Frank, now that he has established himself within the bulwarks of Macklin Enterprises, most likely has his eye set on a distant shimmering horizon of bigger and better resort hotels, office blocks and shopping malls.

And so it goes on, with ambition motivating most fields of human activity in Summer Bay as everywhere else. There are the two town comedians, for instance, who have decided that they will make their fortune by forming themselves into a pop group and are still waiting for their song, recorded with bells and electric guitars with a bit of the surf thrown in, and called 'Santa Never Made It to Summer Bay, to become an instant hit and sweep the charts in a record-breaking way. Celia Stewart is also preparing herself for better things, both in this world and the next.

When I was last in Summer Bay young Steve Mathieson, having abandoned his karate lessons for the time being, was also in the throes of preparation, and going about it in a highly scientific manner. It was young Steve's plan – ambition, if you like – to become a champion with his lips. He wanted to be a topnotch kisser, which accomplishment he was confident would bring him greater success than he is having with the young ladies of the town, but more particularly with one of them whose name is Narelle; his fifteen-year-old heart is pounding wildly in his infatuation for her.

But how to get her to notice him, let alone fall for those charms he knows he possesses but which have yet to flower in full view of this young lady for whom his heart is pounding so wildly? It wasn't good enough just to talk about her to people to the point of boredom, or sigh a lot, pine for her day and night, and follow her with moist and calf-like eyes; he needed to make her sit up and take notice of him, to see him in a new light altogether. So how to do this? How to make possible what at first sight seems impossible?

There is no doubt that Narelle is one of the most bewitching creatures to attend the school at Summer Bay. A tempting creature, and quite voluptuous. Steve was by no means the only young man to become moon-struck over this siren of the coast, but what made it even more difficult for him, put him way back out of sight as it were, was that, at fifteen, he was some years younger than she was. He was just a kid while Narelle was a maturing and very desirable young lady.

That was more or less how Bobby Simpson put it to him when he expressed his unfulfilled desire for the nubile Narelle; he was just a kid, while Narelle had very definite ideas about what to expect from any young man who sought her company, and in one of these, and probably most important, Steve was hardly in the running as aspirant. This was – and here Bobby adopted a tone of awe – that Narelle placed great significance in the quality of the kisses she received, rating them on a scale from one to ten, from bad, indifferent and on upwards to varying degrees of explosive capability. This was why, armed with this interesting information, he set out to fulfil this new ambition of becoming the champion jouster in the kissing tournament, the ace of aces in the sport of love. If Narelle rated kisses on a scale from one to ten, he would break all existing records by opening her eyes to the possibility of a number eleven.

His approach to this was quite methodical. Making the excuse that he was working on a personal development project, he questioned all the girls he knew on this vital subject of The Kiss. He made notes, compared notes, drew up graphs and charts, calculated permutations and radiation content, squared, multiplied, divided and subtracted. To assist him in these studies, he used a ruler, a set of compasses and coloured pencils. He drew and erased and kept amending the parameters already established. He frowned over the circumference of The Kiss, after which it was quite an easy matter to work out its radius. He asked more questions, made more notes and kept a watchful eye out for important common factors.

Before long, and after so much industry, he decided that The Kiss was now in the bag; it was also in the palm of his hand, to be studied and admired in all its many faceted dimensions – and it was a wondrous object that he did behold. But now . . . it had to be put to the test. Narelle had to be asked if she would care to indulge in a little experiment in the cause of Steve's personal development project, whatever that meant.

Narelle being an obliging sort of girl, was only too willing to indulge in this little experiment he had proposed. Kid's stuff, she undoubtedly thought, and it can be assumed that she was quite patronizing about it. But never mind her attitude; that was hardly important now that the chance was here for Steve to bring to bear the fruit of all his feverish researches into the subject of The Kiss.

That moment . . . . ah, to be relished, to be savoured, restored and magnified into legend, from the very first pucker to the final separation of those moist and receptive lips because of the necessity to draw some fresh air down into lungs that had become starved of oxygen. But that moment, in itself so timeless, that perfect moment for the transmission of that perfect kiss that made Narelle gasp and close her eyes in sheer rapture; made her weak at the knees and deliciously shivery afterwards. Never before . . . She opened her eyes to see him as she had never seen him before. Suddenly, the girl was in love with this possessor of The Perfect Kiss who was only fifteen years old. Here she had been, until now, in the vain search for a kiss she could rate as a number ten, and to her delight and without warning had been presented with the totally unexpected bonus of a number eleven, thereby skipping a few grades so far unattained.

It became the talk of the school where Narelle, deciding to throw caution and her misgivings about the damage to her reputation if it became public knowledge that she had been smitten by a fifteen-year-old lip contortionist, demanded a replay of this rapturous event, much to the delight of the onlookers and the enhancement of Steve's own reputation.

So it was that by means of this perfected kiss of his Steve was able to establish himself as a junior Don Juan in Summer Bay – and he played the part to the full. He was cool, he was slick, he was casual, and aware of all the swoony glances that were cast in his direction by the young maidens of the town, most of whom were yet to experience any sort of lip contact beyond the scale of, say, three or four. But Steve only had eyes for the luscious Narelle who felt decidedly weak whenever she was within close range of him, but was already on the look-out for a kiss that could be classified as a number twelve.

The news of Steve's devastating success was quick to spread around the town. What was his secret? The question was asked over and over again, and no one could come up with an answer. When Martin Dibble, one of the town's two comedians and aspiring pop star, and someone who always had his eye open for the main chance, suggested to Steve that a fortune could be made out of his secret if it were marketed properly by means of manuals, booklets, videos, television appearances, shopping mall appearances and the like, Steve rejected it rather loftily by saying that one either had it or didn't have it, it was as simple as that.

But the impermanence of things being the general rule, Steve's notoriety lasted only so long as his kissing grade couldn't be topped, and when a handsome young stranger came to town, Narelle, who still felt compromised a little by her infatuation for a younger man, and was wondering how she might put an end to it, was immediately attracted and had wistful thoughts that here might be the means of achieving a supercharged number twelve on the chart. It also happened that this dark and handsome stranger was Steve's uncle, Phillip Mathieson, who had come to Summer Bay, as he normally did at this time of the year, to cheer up his nephew on the anniversary of his parents' death in the house fire that had orphaned the boy.

So, with Phillip Mathieson's presence in Summer Bay

representing to Narelle the double possibility of shaking off her infatuation for Steve and his Kiss, and the blissful attainment of an even more potent variant, she set to work. But first things being first, she had to ascertain whether Uncle Phillip was capable of producing the fabled number twelve.

In a very natural and impromptu way, she managed to get a foretaste of what he had to offer, by kissing him exuberantly on the cheek, which slightly bemused him, and although it wasn't a kiss of any intensity, nevertheless gave her a pleasant tingling sensation to indicate a lurking potential beneath his darkly handsome exterior – and gave Steve, who witnessed this kiss that seemed so impromptu, a very unpleasant tingling sensation as he felt the ground beginning to slip out from beneath his feet.

But Narelle had to be sure of Phillip's capabilities. She couldn't rest until she was absolutely certain – and it was with this intention in mind that she took a drastic step, in fact those few drastic steps that led up to the first floor of the Fletcher house where Phillip was occupying the spare room. Unable to hold herself back any longer, she rushed into the house early that morning, sprinted up the steps and along the passage to Phillip's room. She wrenched open the door and flung herself onto the bed from where the embodiment of her present ambition was blinking up at her in drowsy surprise.

Narelle was triumphant, it was as she had guessed. She was cured of her crush on Steve once and for all. Steve had been usurped; his number eleven kiss had been surpassed. Narelle had achieved her ambition – for the moment, anyway, because with Steve nursing his bruised ego and already planning refinements to the prototype, her mind was soon turning to the possibilities of a number fourteen, aware, like everyone else, that thirteen is an unlucky number.

A Selected List of Fiction Available from Mandarin

While every effort is made to keep prices low, it is sometimes necessary to increase prices at short notice. Mandarin Paperbacks reserves the right to show new retail prices on covers which may differ from those previously advertised in the text or elsewhere.

The prices shown below were correct at the time of going to press.

All these books are available at your bookshop or newsagent, or can be ordered direct from the publisher. Just tick the titles you want and fill in the form below.

Mandarin Paperbacks, Cash Sales Department, PO Box 11, Falmouth, Cornwall TR10 9EN.

Please send cheque or postal order, no currency, for purchase price quoted and allow the following for postage and packing:

UK   80p for the first book, 20p for each additional book ordered to a maximum charge of £2.00.

BFPO   80p for the first book, 20p for each additional book.

Overseas   £1.50 for the first book, £1.00 for the second and 30p for each additional book
including Eire thereafter.

NAME (Block letters) ....

ADDRESS ....

....

....